Printed in the United States of America

First Printing, 2015

ISBN : 978-0-692-53101-3

www.Amazon.com

CONTENTS

Miss Lovely

Chapter 1

Looking at the beautiful scenery as we make our drive into the Tennessee valley, the trees were so green and full of life. The haze that sat quietly in the mountain tops was like something you would see on a postcard. That fresh mountain air would perk you up after a long drive. The big orange sun was lying peacefully in the clear blue sky.

My brother Kendyle, his son Jayce and I were making the move from Key West Florida to Millington Tennessee. My brothers' wife, Ashley, is in the Navy. They bought a house, nice little ranch home in Tenn. She will be moving bases when she gets back from her third tour overseas. I miss her a lot. We only get to do video chats a couple times a week and a phone call every couple of days. She is out on the ships a lot. I stay with my brother to help take care of Jayce. Kendyle is a lawyer so he works long hours at a time and I'm, well, unemployed at the moment. I never was tied to one career. I have always worked odd end jobs to make ends meet. But last year, Ashley and Kendyle took it upon themselves to send me to college for computer courses. Since I have always been computer savvy, it was a smart move. My brother said he could not stand to see me waste my life away. I plan on paying them back in time though.

"Are you guys ready?" Kendyle says to Jayce and I. "Yeah!" Jayce says with a hyper voice. He has so much energy for a seven year old. He definitely keeps me on my toes. With his bushy black hair and crystal blue eyes, he always makes my day. We pull into the driveway and it really does look like a nice place. The exterior was an ocean blue vinyl with white trim on the windows and doors. The yard was small in the front but well kept. There were little green hedges lining the driveway and the next house was not to close but not too far. Except the house across the street was just how I said, across the street. It seemed like a quiet road but maybe it was because it was on a dead end street. I could hear birds chirping and running water. There must be a creek nearby. This house sat at the end of the road on the right. To the right of our house, was the woods that looked like it ran for miles. And the left a little ways down was a vacant house that was for sale also.

We get out of the car and I stretch my legs since we have been driving for hours. Jayce grabs his dads' keys and runs up to the front porch opening the front door yelling "I have dibs on the best room!" "Hey! Careful buddy! Take your shoes off too!" Kendyle yells. I take a look around the neighborhood from where I am standing. The house across the street really peaks my curiosity. It looks like a mansion from the outside. It has big beautiful bay windows in the front. It's all dark wood and looks freshly stained. The white gravel driveway is lined with yellow tulips. It really made the front of the house stand out. A little silver wind chime hangs right by the wooden porch swing that hovers above the deck that lines the front of the house. It was just gorgeous.

Back in Florida we lived in the very busy part of Key West, everything there was city and a bit dirty. The air was heavy with pollution and humidity. So this will definitely be a well needed change. "Nick?" Kendyle says to me "Yeah." I say turning to face him. "Are you daydreaming?" he says with a laugh. "No. Why? Were you talking to me?" I said with a chuckle. "No, you just seem like you were somewhere." He said with his big white smile.

My brother and I are only a year apart, but he is still my big brother. We could practically be twins. We have been inseparable since we were very young. We resembled one another also; you could tell we were siblings. When we are just hanging out, T-shirts and shorts are our go to clothes. Except when he goes to work, then he cleans up very well in a usually dark grey tux. His hair remains flawless with his wavy short brown flat top hair and big brown eyes.

Where I, on the other hand, just go as I am and sometimes brush my hair when it gets long. Even though I basically just brush it to the side as it falls over one eye most the time. I am due for a trim soon. This pixie cut gets out of control when it's long. "Do you want to unpack first, or you want to show me around?" I asked "Well, help me unhook this trailer so we can get the stuff out of the car. Then I think we should go grab something to eat. I'm pretty hungry." Kendyle said. "Sounds good brother." I said and proceeded to help him with the trailer.

Jayce comes running outside. "Aunt Nicki! You have to check out the back yard! We have a pool with a slide!" Jayce said running to the back yard. "Alright buddy calm down. I'll be there in a sec." I said chuckling shaking my head. "Guess we should teach him to swim huh?" I said in a funny way to Kendyle. "Yeah, guess we should. It might help." Kendyle said. "It just might." I smirked. As I am holding the trailer while Kendyle tried pulling the pin out. "Can you lift it up a little higher; the pin is wedged in there." Kendyle said starting to perspire. He was a small thin guy but he packed some muscle.

I had that feeling like someone was watching us from the beautiful house across the street. I turn to look, but I see no one at a glance. Then I turn again to get a better look. I notice one of the downstairs curtains was pulled back with a slight. As if someone is watching us but keeping a distance as not to be seen. I shrug it off as a nosey neighbor turning back to face Kendyle. "This damn thing." Kendyle said getting aggravated. "Do we have any seven eleven in the trunk?" I asked. "I'm not sure sis, you can check." He said giving it a rest for a moment as he stayed crouched on the ground wiping the sweat from his forehead with the bottom of his muscle shirt.

I popped the trunk and took a few boxes out to make things a little more accessible. "I'm not seeing any bro." as I still sifted through a box from our old garage. "Okay," as he took a deep breath "Let's give it another try. Maybe push down of the arm." He said. I sat on the arm of the trailer pushing all my weight into it. As I struggled giving it all I had, I said jokingly "Try to make it snappy huh." Kendyle looked up at me with a "yeah right" grin. "Just for that I'll take my time." He said trying to make humor of our situation. I hear the echo of a door close from behind me. I take a quick glance and that was the first time I saw Gracie Lovely.

She stood on her porch putting her slip on black flat shoes, pulling the elastic backing of the shoe out to slip her heel in. As she walked down the three stairs on the porch it was all in slow motion for me. I even had a song in my head *Got you*, By the Flys. As she made her way towards us she was stunning.

Her long loosely curled dark brown hair, brushed her face as a gentle late summer breeze made an entrance. She ran her hand through her hair to whisk it to one side out of her face. She kept her head slightly down watching where she was walking. Her light blue short shorts helped the bright evening sun shine off her golden tanned legs. Her black spaghetti stringed top revealed a sexy black lace bra underneath. I'm pretty sure it was a push up, judging from the way her breasts made a perfect V shape in the middle of her chest.

As I am mesmerized by what I believe to had been an angel that just descended on earth, I can hear the muffled sound of my brothers voice. "Nick, a little higher...Nick!" he said. "Hmm. What?" I said as if I just snapped out of a trance looking back at Kendyle. "Umm what are you looking at?" he said. Before I could answer we hear a "Hello, I'm Gracie Lovely!" she said in an innocent but yet excited voice like she hasn't seen anyone in months. I turn around and Kendyle stood up. "Hey..." I said smiling. Jayce comes running outside. "Daddy! I'm hungry." Jayce says running over to us. "Well, aren't you the most handsome young man ever!" Gracie said bent slightly over to Jayce. "Good looks must run in the family." She added looking at me giving me a wink.

Her soft desert brown eyes glistened in the sun which made them look almost like a deep hunter green. Her high cheek bones accented her perfectly round eyes. They were so pretty I couldn't stop staring in them. She was naturally beautiful, not even a drop of make-up was on. "Oh," I chuckled as I walked over to Jayce. "Well I'm his aunt and that's his dad Kendyle, my brother." I said putting my hand on Jayce's back. "Nice to meet you Miss Lovely." Kendyle said waving and putting his hands on his hips waiting on me to get back to helping him. "Please, call me Gracie. Whenever someone calls me Miss I feel so old." She said with a chuckle. "And you are?" Gracie said smiling turning her attention back at me "I'm sorry, I'm Nicole but you can call me Nicki or Nick." I said feeling embarrassed. I could feel my ears burning at this point.

"So are you guys just staying awhile?" she said looking at our small trailer that only had a few essential things on it and Jayce's bike. "Why do you say that?" I asked. "Because from the looks of your trailer, it seems that you are going on a camping trip." She said giggling. "Oh!" I said laughing nervously. "No, we are waiting on the movers. They should be here sometime next week." I said still grinning. "You two will make good friends." Kendyle said sarcastically. "Oh yeah! Why is that?" Gracie asked. "Because you both are smart asses." He said smiling. "You will have to excuse him, he is a bit cranky." I said looking back at Kendyle sticking my tongue at him. "It's understandable, moving can be a bit stressful." She said interlocking her hands together putting them in front of her. "Do you guys need any help?" she asked. "Do you have anything to get this pin out?" Kendyle asked pointing at the hinge. She walked closer to the trailer as she put her hand through her hair again. "What would you need?" she asked. "Hammer will do." He said. "Yeah, I have something that will help you there. My father had a bunch of tools that still linger in the garage. I'll be right back." She said running over to her house. "Hey sis, wipe that drool from your mouth." Kendyle said laughing. "Oh my god! Right?! She is gorgeous!" I said quietly walking over to him. "She is pretty. Ask her out." He said grinning. "What? No way dude. We just got here. I'll give it some time first. Till then, at least I have something to look at." I said looking back at her house. "And stalk." Kendyle said jokingly. "Whatever man." I said.

Gracie jogs back over with a sledge hammer holding it in both hands. "Will this do?" she asks putting her hand through her hair again whisking it back to one side. Another gentle breeze came and I could smell the cherry blossom being extracted from her golden skin. Kendyle gave the pin two good hits and out it came. "Thank you Gracie." He said handing her the hammer back. "Anytime! If you guys need anything else, never hesitate to ask. My door is always open." She said with an innocent smile. "Ours too." I said as she looked at me with those electrifying eyes. "Well I will see you guys later. I know you probably have a lot to do." She said getting ready to walk away.

"Hey" Kendyle said. Gracie turned around quickly. "Is there any good pizza places around here. I have to feed these guys." Kendyle said giving me a friendly nudge. "Most definitely there is! It's about fifteen minutes from here. It's called Capella's. If you go to the end of this road make a left and just go straight it will be on your right." She said "Do they have wings?" Jayce asked excited. "Well of course! What kind of pizza place doesn't have wings?" she said in a playful voice. "Can we go there daddy?" Jayce turned to Kendyle. "Of course bud, go change your shirt first." Kendyle said. Gracie continued to walk to her house. "You can join us." Kendyle said loudly as Gracie was in her yard. I turned and looked at Kendyle as he gave me a grin. "She can?" I whispered as I wasn't too sure because we just met her. Kendyle has always been cautious of new people. "Yeah, why not?" He whispered back to me. "You don't mind? I don't want to be a bother." Gracie yelled from across the street. "Don't be silly. Come on." Kendyle said waving her back over. "Okay!" she said locking her house and making her way back over to our car.

We sat in silence for a moment as Kendyle pulled out of the driveway. I didn't want the ride to be awkward, so I tried to make small talk. "Your house is gorgeous!" I said turning around to face her and Jayce in the back seat. "Thank you. I try to keep it looking nice." She says. "Do you have any animals?" Jayce asked with excitement. "Why yes I do! I have a cat, his name is Cloud." She said smiling at Jayce. Jayce began to laugh. "That's a funny name." he said still laughing. "It is different." Kendyle said looking in the rearview at Gracie. "Well you would understand if you saw him. He is huge and his fur is very fluffy. He does look like a cloud with eyes." She said snickering holding her hands up to her face making open fits for eyes. Jayce continued to laugh.

We arrive at Capella's, and it's a very small parlor in a shopping plaza with Navaho blankets hanging on a banister outside. "This sure is different than back home." Kendyle said opening the door for us. "Where are you guys from?" Gracie asked as we walked in. "Well we just came from Florida but we grew up in Ohio." I said to Gracie. "My wife is in the navy. So we move a lot." Kendyle added walking to a table. "That is great. I love seeing strong women. It's empowering." Gracie said sitting next to me. "Where are you from? You don't have a southern accent like most of the folks here." Kendyle said. "Believe it or not I was born here. But I did spend a lot of time in Oregon till I moved back here a few years ago." She replied. "So what do you do for a living?" she asked Kendyle changing the subject abruptly. "I'm a lawyer." He said situating Jayce. "No, he is being modest. He is the top dog lawyer in Florida." I said sternly. "Yeah yeah." Kendyle said smiling.

"What made you want to be a lawyer?" she asked. "Uhm, honestly, when Nick and I were growing up, I remember seeing this guy on trial for murdering his family, but he was proven innocent and let go of all charges because the prosecutor wasn't very good at what he did. It just really made me mad that no one could see this man deserved to rot in hell. So I decided it was my calling to put scum like him away for good." He said. "You seem so young to be a lawyer." She said. "Thank you. I am only thirty. I haven't been doing it long but I've had some much credited cases that have made me pretty high in demand." He added. "How bout' you?" Gracie nudged my shoulder. "I'm just a house Aunt at the moment." I laughed "But I am doing online courses for computer software." I said "So, you are really good with computers?" she asked. "I'm decent." I said chuckling. "Now I know who to call when my laptop is malfunctioning." She said with a laugh. "Ghostbuster?" I said making a joke. "That's exactly who I was thinking of." Gracie laughed. "What about you? What do you do for a living?" I asked. "I work from home. I do flower arrangements." She said. "Really? Is it your own business kind of thing?" I asked. "Yeah, something like that." She said. "I have a huge greenhouse in the backyard that I grow all kinds of flowers in." she added. "Do you live alone?" Kendyle asked. "Yes I do." She said getting fidgety like she was getting nervous. "Sorry, It's just you have such a beautiful home and you are an attractive young woman, I thought maybe you were living there with family or something." Kendyle added. She smiled and replied "Thank you. I am blessed with young skin." She said smirking. "It was my parents' house, but they passed away about twenty years ago and I inherited all of it. I grew up in that house. I just cannot get myself to sell it. So I decided to stay there." She continued.

I looked at her from my peripheral trying to not make it obvious that I was. "If you don't mind me asking, how old are you?" Kendyle asked. "How old do you think I am?" she said with a devious grin. "Oh man, that question coming from a woman makes me nervous." Kendyle said jokingly. "Nick, how bout you take this one." He said laughing. "Hmmm, Well, you have a young face, but the way you carry yourself and talk, I am going to say our age so thirty ish?" I said turning slowly to look at Gracie. "You are very observant." Gracie said looking at me seductively. "You are close, I am thirty five." She answered. "Wow! I hope I look that good in five years!" Kendyle said surprised. "Yeah! No joke!" I added. Gracie smiled flattered. "You guys are too nice." She said starting to blush. It was cute the way her cheeks had a little hint of pink from my brother and I's flattery.

CHAPTER 2

The next morning the first thing I did was search for places hiring on my phone. Sundays are always the best for that. "Nick?" I hear my brother call me from the other room. "In here." I said. "Hey, what are you doing?" Kendyle says walking into the room. "Just searching for jobs." I said. "I start mine tomorrow, I thought I had a week off but my old boss just called and told me I have to go in tomorrow." Kendyle explained. "It's all good Brother; I'll take Jayce to school no worries." I said with a smile. "I know. You are so awesome sis, I'm glad you decided to stick around. You definitely help with the load I have." Kendyle said. "I am pretty great." I smiled. "How far is Jayce's school?" I asked. "I typed it in the Navi and I left it on the counter. So you are good to go for the morning. It's not too far. Fifteen minutes to walk it I think." He said. "That's not too bad." I said. "My work on the other hand is forty five minutes." He laughs. "Oooo early birdy you're gonna be grumpy." I said smiling. "I'll be gone when you get up." he says with a sarcastic smirk as he walks back down the hall. "It's better for all of us!" I yell with a chuckle. "Whatev!" Kendyle says off in the distance.

I hear rustling around outside, and I see Kendyle unloading the trailer and the car. I go out to help him taking a break from my job search. "Hey, why didn't you say something?" I asked walking to grab a box. "You looked very engrossed with what you were doing." Kendyle says sarcastically. "Well if you really want to do this all by yourself." I said starting to walk away. "Since you are out

14

here..." Kendyle says humorously. "That's what I thought."
I laughed.

As we finally emptied the SUV and trailer, we sat on the front porch to chill out for a minute. "I didn't realize we could fit so much stuff in that Escalade." I said surprised. "Well the hard part is done!" Kendyle says. "Umm yeah. Now we have to unpack and arrange the house." I said. "That is supposed to be the fun part." Kendyle replied. "For who!?" I said surprised. He laughed. "I guess you will be the one doing all that since I have to go to work." Kendyle added. "Since I don't have a job." I said. "If you are bored you have something to do till you get a job." Kendyle joked. "I see. You won't like the way I arrange it." I said laughing. "Jayce, get in the house and wash up, you are filthy." Kendyle said. "Okay pops." Jayce said and went inside. "Where did he get that from?" Kendyle asked me. "Uhm I don't know. You let him watch weird old movies. Maybe from there." I said sarcastically. Kendyle gave me look and pinched my arm. "Ouch you crab cake!" I said putting him in a head lock. We wrestled around in the front yard.

Gracie watched from her living room window behind the white curtains. She maintained a grin that could only be described as intrigued. "Say I am the best!" I said to Kendyle as I had a good grip on him still. In a playful manner he gasped for air. "Ahhh! You are the best!" he yelled jokingly. I released him from my grips. He gave me a punch on the arm. "Punk" he said catching his breath. "I'll get you next time!" he added. "That's what you always say." I said jokingly. Kendyle stood there for a moment still trying to catch his breath. I stuck my tongue out at him. "I think you are getting too old for this playing around." I said laughing. "Am not!" Kendyle said in disgust humorously. "Are you going to staying out here for a bit?" Kendyle asks. "Yeah I'll be in in a few. Why? Do you need a nap now" I said grinning ear to ear awaiting another attack from him. "Ha Ha, very funny smart ass." He said giving me a glare as he proceeded to the porch. Kendyle shut the door and I just took in the outside fresh air.

I felt eyes on me as I sat on the porch, leaning on the top stair. I tried not to make it obvious that I knew someone was looking at me so I tried to be really slick. I got up and started walking around the house pretending I was looking around at the landscape that outlined our yard. I found some tall hedges that were slightly taller than me on the side of the house leading to the back yard, to where Gracie wouldn't be able to see me looking over there. I have to admit I felt a little like a creep for doing this, but I didn't know why she was acting shy since we formally met yesterday.

Then she came out and stood on her porch. I made my way back to the front yard. She walked over to our house. Her hair was wrapped up into a perfect bun and she was wearing a see through red blouse that had a matching kami underneath. "Hey Gracie!" I said acting surprised. "Hey!" she said in a happy voice. She was holding a silver flat platter that had tin foil covering the contents underneath. "What do you have there?" I asked smiling. "Well I saw you and your brother were working hard over here. So I made you guy's cookies. I hope you like peanut

16

butter." She said grinning handing them to me. I could smell that fresh peanut butter before I even lifted the foil. "Of course! We love cookies here!" I said taking the tray making an opening in the foil to grab one. The platter was so warm as if I were taking one out of the oven. "Peanut butter is my favorite!" I exclaimed. "Did you guys get everything in the house?" She asked putting her hands in the back pockets of her bleached jean shorts. "Just what we have yeah. But, there is a whole truck load coming Friday." I said stuffing the cookie in my mouth. "Moving is so stressful." She said watching me eat the cookie. "Yeah, we are used to it though. Military life." I said. "Thank you so much for these, they are awesome. " I said having another cookie. "I can tell." She said smiling not taking her eyes off me. "Would you like to come in?" I asked. "I'd love to!" she said happily.

We walked in and Kendyle was standing in the kitchen trying to get his laptop charged. "Look what our neighbor brought us!" I said setting the tray on the counter. "Cookies!?" Kendyle said excited grabbing the one I had in my hand gobbling it down. "Hey!" I said pinching his arm. "That one was mine punk." I said putting my fist up in a playful manner. "I want a cookie!" Jayce yelled from the bathroom. "After your bath buddy." Kendyle yelled back. "Thank you Gracie, that was really nice of you." He said grabbing another going back to his laptop.

Gracie started to walk around. "This house is so beautiful." She said looking in the living room. We had a fireplace and new white carpet. It was quite homey. "Thank you. My wife really wanted it." He said. "Well, she has great taste." Gracie said turning back around to face us. "That she does." I said. "So Gracie, do you like card games." Kendyle asked. "I love games." She said folding her hands together in front of her. "Sweet. I have Uno. We were gonna play a game. Would you like to join us?" I asked as I knew Kendyle didn't mind. "Sure!' she said. Kendyle went to get Jayce out of the tub. "I'll be back in a sec." he said.

Gracie and I sat in the living room on the floor Indian style since we didn't have any furniture yet. "I love your shorts." Gracie said to me. "Thank you. They are Hurley." I said touching the material. She put her hand on my shorts to feel them also. 'They are so soft." She said looking at me. I hesitated as she gave me a bit of a jolt through my body. "Uhm yeah they are....dry fit." I said almost forgetting what we were even talking about. She giggled and put her hand back in her lap. Kendyle and Jayce joined us for a game.

Later on that night I walked her back to her house. "I had fun, thank you for letting me hang out with you guys." She said. "Anytime girl." I said. She gave me a hug, putting her arms around my neck and I put mine around her waist. She gave a good squeeze and I could smell that sweet scent of cherry blossom again. I swear it made me melt. When she pulled away she stood so close I thought she was going to kiss me. I could feel her breath tickle my nose. "I'll see you later?" she asked. "Definitely." I said. As I walked off the porch, she watched me walk to my house as I turned around before walking in. She smile then waved at me. I smiled back then proceeded inside.

When I walked back into the living room Jayce had the laptop in his lap and Kendyle sitting next to him. "There she is." Kendyle said in a funny voice. "We get to see mommy!" Jayce said excited. Ashley must be on land today. It's the only time we get to talk to her which, lately those days have been few and far between. I sat down next to Jayce and kissed his head. "Are you excited?" I asked Jayce. "Yup!" he said with a huge smile nodding his head excitedly.

These few moments were always so nerve racking. It was like watching a suspense film. Finally her chat call arrived. "Hey!!" we could hear Ashley but no picture yet. There is always a thirty second delay which was irritating but doable. "Hi mommy!!" Jayce excitedly replied. Kendyle and I always let Jayce do the talking for the first ten minutes. Otherwise we wouldn't be able to hear a thing Ashley says. "Hey baby, I miss you so much! You are getting so big." She said almost tearing up. She hasn't been home to see us in nine months. But it feels like years. Her natural blonde hair was always pulled into a ponytail. Her crystal blue eyes were identical to Jayce's. She had best posture too. I always envied that about my sis in law. As long as we have known her, she was confident and it showed just by looking at her. I wish I had that discipline growing up so I wasn't so used to slouching. "I miss you too mommy! This house is so cool! We have a pool and a slide that goes into it!" Jayce said. "Yeah! I guess daddy and aunt Nicki will have to show you how to swim huh?" she said smiling. "Yeah! I'm excited!" he added. "I can tell baby." She replied with a little laugh. "Are you helping daddy and Auntie Nicki with moving?" she asked. "Of

19

course mama!" he said with a snicker. "Good boy. What did you have for dinner today?" she asked making small talk. "A cookie!" he said smiling. "A cookie huh?" As she gave us all a joking glare.

Kendyle put his hands up like he was surrendering with his huge white smile. I just shrugged and smiled. "Well I guess when I get home, I have some spanking to do." She said playfully. "Mommy?" Jayce asked. "Yes baby." She said. "When are you coming home?" he said. Ashley paused. She always hates that question because she doesn't know the answer. "Honey, I will be home really soon okay? Listen, just think of this. When I get home this time, I'm staying home. I won't have to leave for months at a time anymore. You will see me every night. Okay sweetheart?" she said holding the tears back. Jayce nodded his head yes and cried in silence as he laid his head on my side.

I put my arm around him, laying my head on his. "I love you Jayce." She added. "I love you too mommy." Jayce said wiping his eyes. He handed the laptop to Kendyle. "Hey sexy." Kendyle said with a big grin. "Hey sis." I added. "Hey my two trouble makers. Are you guys getting settled?" she smiled. "We are working on it." I said. "I cannot wait till you get home. You know how sexy that uniform makes you look." Kendyle smirked. "You better stop that. I'm miles away Mr. Shaw." She said with a wink. She is an O-6 captain which is pretty impressive for someone as young as her. She wore three pins, Command at sea, Command ashore/project manager, and The SEAL trident on the left side of her uniform. Above that she had her ribbons sown on neatly. I could go on for hours of all the ribbons she had but the one she is most proud of is her Combat action ribbon and the Presidential unit citation. She was very humble about all her accomplishments. I love when she comes home and tells us stories. It reminds me when my father would come home and tell us about all the places he would visit being in the air force.

I cleared my throat. "Excuse me. Can you two take that somewhere else please?" I said in a joking way. "Jealous?" Kendyle said sarcastic. "You wish." I winked. "How is school going sis?" Ashley asked. "My summer courses were good. I received three A's and one B. I'm very proud." I said with confidence. "That is fantastic!" she said. "Are they keeping their word on bring you back in November?" Kendyle asked. "So far babe. Everything is still kind of rocky here. But, they tell us we should be able to be home for Thanksgiving." She said. "That would be great." I added. "Yes it would. What I would give for some turkey and stuffing right now." She said in a yearning manner. "I'll give you some stuffing." Kendyle said winking. "Ew daddy!" Jayce yelled. "Really? In front of your son." I whispered but smiled because it was funny. "Dyle, I got something special for you when I get home." Ashley replied with a vixen grin. "Oh my. I do not want to hear any of this man." I said standing up with Jayce. Ashely and Kendyle started laughing. They do this stuff even when they are here together. I always loved that about them though. Its real love like our parents had when they were around. "Jayce, I want you to be careful around that pool okay? It's deep at one end." She said seriously. "I will mommy." Jayce replied. "Dyle, buy him some floats or something." She said. "I will sexy." He said with a big grin. "Well my loves, I have to go." She kisses the screen. "I love you guys. I will see you soon." She said. "We love you too." We all said in sync. "Bye." She whispered as she started to tear up and the screen went black.

I picked Jayce up and carried him to his room. Kendyle followed us. We tucked Jayce in lying on both sides of him on the bed while he fell asleep. It helps him I think after he has talked to Ashley.

CHAPTER 3

Monday morning came so fast. I heard Kendyle fumbling around which woke me. I didn't have to get up for another two hours with Jayce. But I laid there on my mattress on the floor. I heard Kendyle leave and I must have dozed back off because I woke up to my alarm.

I get Jayce up and rolling. I packed his lunch while making a little breakfast for him and I. "Are you ready for a new school?" I asked him. "Yeah." He said in a sad way. "What's wrong bud?" I asked. "Just new people." Jayce said looking at me with those little puppy blue eyes. "I know sweetheart. But it's a part of life we all go through it. Your dad and I had to go to a lot of different schools because Grandpa Shaw had a job like mommy does." I said. "Really?" Jayce said with a little more spark. "Yes sir. You just be yourself and go with the flow." I said smiling kissing his forehead. "Time to go buddy. We have a little bit of a walk." I said grabbing his book bag and the Navi.

I walk Jayce to school but he stops at the stairs leading up to the building. I think we were both taken back by how big the school was. Jayce looked up like he was staring at skyscrapers. I turn to him and kneel down. "I'll be here to get you at two okay?" I said. Jayce shook his head yes as a teacher came walking down the stairs to us. Her gold framed glasses hugged the middle of her nose gently. Her grey short puffy hair looked like a cotton ball. I bet if I were to touch it, it would be super soft. "Hello! You must be the Shaw's'?" She asked with a southern drawl and huge smile. "Yes ma'am. I'm Nick and this is Jayce." I said. "Jayce is a handsome name." she said to Jayce.

"Thank you." Jayce said hiding behind me slightly. She was so polite. She reminded me of my grandma so elegant and big hearted. She stuck her hand out to Jayce to make him more comfortable. "I'll walk you to your class Jayce." She said with a smile. "It's okay. I'll see you later. I love you." I said kissing his cheek. "I Love you too aunt Nicki." Jayce said taking the teachers hand. As they walked into the school, Jayce kept looking behind him to see if I was still standing there. I waved till he turned the corner to walk into the school. I felt a bit sad, but in a good way.

When I arrived home, I started to unpack some boxes. About fifteen minutes into it I hear a knock at the door. "Hey!" Gracie said with a big smile. "I hope I'm not interrupting you." She said. "Not at all. Want to come in?" I said moving to the side so she could. "You will have to excuse the mess though." I added. "I came over to ask if you could look at my computer. It's freezing up on me and I have to get a few orders done." she asks uncertainly. "Yeah! I'd be happy to help you." I said smiling. I shut the door behind me making my way across the street with Gracie.

As I walk in, it looked totally different from what I had imagined it would look like. Everything was so neat and modern. It smelled like vanilla with a hint of Lysol as if she just finished cleaning. There were so many directions you could walk. To the left was a darken room that looks like she doesn't use. It had a huge dining room table in it with a bouquet of fake red flowers that sat on a white doily perfectly in the middle. There was a china cupboard that sat against the wall in the back that was filled with what

24

looked like very expensive plates, bowls and wine glasses. If I had to guess, it was just for decoration. In front of me was a beautiful wooden staircase that led to the upstairs, with a crystal chandelier hanging from the ceiling in the hallway. Then next to the staircase was the hallway to the kitchen and sliding doors that led to the back deck. To my right was the living room that had a huge TV mounted on the wall, a white leather sectional couch, and a grey stone fireplace that sat under the middle of the TV. The mantle that encased the fireplace had two porcelain angels siting upon it holding each other's hands. There was a white door that sat back on the right side of the living room. I think it was for the garage. Then there was an open door on the left side that was the office.

"Wow. This place is beautiful." I said looking around in awe. "You have this all to yourself?" I asked with a chuckle. "Yeah just me and Cloud." She said picking up a big white cat as she kisses his nose. "He is a cutie and does look like a cloud with eyes." I said petting his head chuckling. I looked up locking eyes with Gracie for a moment as she smiled and said "My computer is in here." as she walked me through the hallway I noticed a dark wooden door hidden under the staircase. Then as we entered the kitchen there was another hallway to my left. "This house goes on forever" I said jokingly. "There is a lot of space." She said turning around to look at me. She led me to the left to a room off from the living room.

I sat down and worked my magic. I fixed her problem in minutes. "Wow. That was fast! You do know what you are doing." She chuckles. "I know a little somethin' somethin'" I said brushing my shoulder off. "If your cache is filled up, it will freeze frequently." I told her. "Thank you so much." She said. "Really, it was no problem." I said walking over to the front door. "Enjoy the rest of your day Gracie." I said as I walked back to my house. I could feel Gracie watching me walk away even till I closed the door behind me. I peeked through the curtain on the door to see if she was still watching. I couldn't see any evidence but that's not to say she was being discrete about it.

About an hour passes and another knock was at the door. I whispered to myself "Who is it now?" as I walked quickly to the door. I swung it open and it was Gracie yet again. "Miss me already huh?" I said jokingly. "Am I that obvious?" she said mischievously. "Just a little." I chuckled. "Can you come take a look at this thing that keeps popping up on my screen? I think I may have downloaded a virus of some sort by accident." She said smiling. "Sure." I said quietly as it kind of made me start thinking she just wanted me over there.

I walk back in to the room with the computer. "Are you talking about this?" I said pulling it up from the tab bar. She stood behind me leaning down to my ear as she said softly "Yes. It keeps flashing and I don't know why." As I could feel her breath on my ear, it gave me chills. Her soft bedroom voice radiated through my head like church bells. I even had goosebumps. I know she could see them on my arm since it was on the desk controlling the mouse. I didn't want to draw attention so I acted as if I didn't notice them.

I could feel her glancing at my arm then smiling in a seductive way as she stood back up. "Well" I said almost choking on my spit clearing my throat "Sorry, wrong pipe." As I coughed a good one to clear my throat of the frog. "No apologies." She whispered as she ran her fingertips along my right shoulder then to my back to my left shoulder. Resting her hand on my left shoulder. "This is just to remind you that there is an update for your order program. Would you like to update it?" I asked as I turned my head to look up at her. "Yes I would." She softly spoke as we locked eyes again. They glistened from the sun beams shining in from the bay windows. When the sun hits them they had a light brown sugar color. They made my mouth water; I was seriously hoping I wouldn't drool.

"Okay." I softly said back, smiled and proceeded to download it for her. "This may take a few minutes but when this, I mean it's done just restart the computer and you... I mean the program will be all new." I said fumbling on my words getting up almost tripping over the roller chair. "Watch yourself." Gracie smiled walking closer to me. "There is a chair there." I said walking backwards slowly to the door. I stopped in the doorway of the office. "Thank you." She said as we stood gazing at each other. "Anytime." I said laughing under my breath. "Well, I should get back, I have some unpacking to do." I said breaking the silence. "You can come back after you are done." She replied. "Okay, I will keep that in mind." I smiled and walked myself out.

Later that day I pick up Jayce from school. "How was your first day?" I asked. "It was Okay." He said with his head down. "You want to talk about it?" I asked sensing something was off. "No." He said. I grabbed his head and pulled him close to me to hug him. "How does ice cream sound for a before dinner snack?" I asked with a grin. "Yeah!" Jayce's' face lite up. "Okay, don't tell your dad though. He will kick my butt." I said "Secret is safe with me sister!" he said with a chuckle. As I grabbed the Navi the battery was dead. "We have to go across the street first bud. I am not sure where one is at around here." I said as we went to Gracie's.

I knocked softly on her front door. Jayce looked up at me and gave me a big grin. She answered quickly as it kind of startled me. "Your back!" she said excited. "I am! I came to ask if there are any places to get an ice cream around here." I asked. She giggled and replied "Of course silly. There is a creamery. But it's kind of a walk. It's in town." She said "Damn, like how far?" I asked. "Twenty minutes tops. I could drive you guys there." She said. "That would be great! I was going to ask you if you wanted to join us anyways." I said with a smile. "I'd love to go with you two." She said. "Great!" I said.

Gracie's car was immaculate. I mean the wax on this car I could probably slide right off the damn thing. I think this chick is obsessed with vanilla. Her car had that scent along with a small hint of the garage mixed in. The cool leather seats felt nice on my back since it was a bit of a scorcher today. "Thanks again for taking us. He had a rough first day at school I think." I said softly. "Oh no." Gracie said softly back. "Ice cream will always make things better." Gracie added and smiled at me.

We arrived at the creamery. It was so little compared to what we were used to in Key West. But in a way it was kind of nice because I always hated the crowds and the wait. We walk in as Jayce runs to the window to look at all the different flavors. "Aunt Nicki! They have superman flavor!" he said excited. "They do huh! Guess I know what you're getting then." I replied. "Two scoops!" he said holding up two fingers. "Hungry little man." Gracie said smiling. "What kind is your favorite?" I asked Gracie. "I love vanilla" she said. "I wouldn't have guessed that." I said sarcastically. She gave me a friendly push. "Think you are funny, do ya?" she jokingly replied. "I have my moments." I said smirking. "I'm buying so do it up girl." I said nudging her shoulder. "How nice of you." She replied. I had a little money left from my job back in Florida.

The chick behind the counter made Jayce's first. "May I have sprinkles?" Jayce asked the girl. "Of course!" she replied. Then when it was my turn she said "He is adorable! How old is he?" With a southern drawl. It was cute. She was young, maybe early twenties. Blonde hair and blue eyes with a red hat on that said Cris's Creamery on it. Her hair pulled through the snap in the back. "Thank you. He is seven. He will be eight in a couple of months." I replied with a smile. "He will definitely be a knockout with those blue eyes when he gets older." She said watching Jayce get messy with his ice cream. "Jayce, get a napkin." I said a bit embarrassed. "Y'all are not from here huh?" she asked. "Did I give it away?" I said with a chuckle. "Kind of." She giggled. I could see from the corner of my eye Gracie glaring at this girl. I wasn't sure of the deal. "I love your shirt! I only have been to Cali once, it was gorgeous."

She explained talking about my made in Cali T-shirt I had on. "Thank you. I love it there too." I said feeling a little nervous now that I could see the blank expression on Gracie's face. "Hey" I said nudging Gracie. "Are you Okay?" I whispered as the chick was waiting on Gracie to give her the order for her ice cream. "Yes. I am totally fine." She said still glaring at the chick behind the counter not batting a lash, but maintaining a smile. I didn't say anything else as I paid for our bowls.

We sat at a table in the corner to enjoy our ice cream. I just couldn't help but to look at Gracie's eyes. They were just so beautiful. The shape was perfect the color was glistening it was like I was looking at a mural painting of an angel. It was a breath of fresh air. It made me forget to ask her about the mishap at the counter.

We make it back to the house just before Kendyle arrived home. "Thank you again for taking us. I know I probably said that a million times already but I really mean it." I said. "No problem. Anytime you guys want to do it again I'm for the company. I don't get many visitors." She said. "Well I have to get him back before Kendyle pulls in." I said '"It's a secret we went today. Kendyle doesn't like it when I spoil dinner." I said with a laugh. "Your secret is safe with me." She said locking her lips with a key motion. "Hey, let me see your phone real quick." Gracie said. "My phone?" I said confused. I didn't know what she was gonna do with it. I took it out of my pocket and handed it to her. She smiled putting her number in it with a smiley emoji at the end. "There, now you can text me when you want to come hang out." She winked, handing me back the phone. "Sweet. Will do." I smiled as we made our way back to the house.

Gracie waits till sundown, then heads back out to the creamery. She sits across the street waiting for the young lady to get off work. Finally the blonde leaves the building with Gracie following far behind. The young lady pulls into some run down apartments as Gracie keeps her distance across the street. The blonde gets out of her car gathering her things. Gracie abruptly comes up behind her placing a plastic bag over the blondes face suffocating her. The blonde struggles trying to grab Gracie. Gracie trips her to the ground knocking the blonde out of breath. Gracie puts her knee in her back making it impossible for the blonde to fight. As she gasps for air the bag takes her life. The place was gloomy and dark. There were no street lamps and no one seemed to be around. After the blonde takes her last breath, Gracie takes the bag and runs off.

CHAPTER 4

As Jayce and I make our way to school the next
day, Gracie watched from her living room window as we
turned the corner of the street. She elegantly walked over to
our house and slowly up the porch stairs. She took a bobbie
pin out of her perfectly pinned up hair looking around. She
then picked the lock letting herself in. As she strolled
through the house she ran her fingers along the wall leading
to the bedrooms.

The sun caught her face as she passed by each room
till she reached mine. She stood in the doorway, closing her
eyes and inhaled a deep breath as if she were taken into
euphoria from my scent. She maintained a closed mouth
grin as she looked around the room. The room was still
packed up. A mattress rested on the floor with a heavy
comforter on it. With a small drawer type desk next to it.
She came across a box that had picture frames, as she
grabbed the first one on top that was faced down. She
picked it up. It was a picture of me and my best friend Sam.
Gracie traced her fingers along my face in the picture then
flipped it over taking the picture out placing it in her bra.
Then placing the frame back the way it was before she
picked it up. She walked over to a book bag full of clothes
and picked a few shirts out holding them up to her nose
inhaling deeply, then folded them nicely to put them back
in.

She came across a box labeled *Fragile*. She kneeled
down next to it, opened it up as the flaps of the box were
just folded amongst one another. The first thing she saw
was a plastic toy heart that wore sunglasses and had its

thumbs up with a big smile. On the back of it read *I love you*. She placed it into her black sweater pocket, as she sifted more into the box. There were a few things in there from Kendyle. Like a snow globe with the two of us in it that read *The best sis ever. Love your big bro.* There was a glass picture frame that had little pictures of the family in it. She smiled then folded the box back up. My laptop was on my mattress; she picked it up and inserted a small chip into one of my USB ports. She put it back down the way she found it. She began to make her way to the front door and left. Just as Gracie closes her front door, I arrive onto the porch of our house.

Just as I am settling in, I have an eerie feeling. As if someone has been in the house. I looked around my room from sitting on my mattress, but nothing looked misplaced. Not that I would really notice anyways since things were still a mess. So I search the house just in case I am not alone. Upon finding nothing, I shrug it off as the new house nerves. I find a job that is right down the road from Jayce's school. It's a coffee café looking for bussers and waitresses. I apply in hopes that it would be the perfect job since it's all in walking distance.

I soon, thereafter get a video chat request from my best friend Samantha that lives in Florida. "Hey girl!" I say excited. "I miss you so damn much already!" Sam says. "I know, damn me and my love for my bro right?" I said with a laugh. "Nothing to be ashamed about girl. I wish I had your guy's relationship with my siblings." She said. "So how are the boys?" I asked "Well" she says grabbing one of them to bring them in the web cam view. "This one

almost got suspended on the first day of school already."
She said hugging her eldest. "What did you do Gavin?" I
said "I hit this stupid kid." He said. "Why?" I asked
"Because he was causing drama." He replied. "Drama?
Your only ten dude." I said and laughed. "Yeah, well I had
to leave work and everything I was not a happy mom
today." Sam said with a discerning look. "I bet you
weren't." I said smiling. "So are you still coming up?" I
asked "Hell yeah girl! I could use a little vacation! That is
the only good thing about you moving away." She said
laughing. "Are the boys coming too?" I asked smiling.
"Hell no! Their grandma is going to watch them." She said.
"So we can be bad girls?" I said grinning. "You know I
always am." Sam said with a wink. "Speaking of bad girls,
have you heard from Kristen?" she asked. "No thank
goodness. She only texted me once since we been here but I
haven't responded." I said. "What did it say?" she asked.

Meanwhile Gracie sits in front of her computer
glaring at her screen watching me and Sam have this video
chat. Her fist is up to her expressionless face. She clenches
her fist together leaving indentations on her palm. Biting
down on her back teeth breathing heavily.

I pick up my phone to read the text out loud to Sam
in a slutty voice. "Hey baby, just wanted you to know, no
matter what you will always be my one. I know I messed
up, but I was hoping you could look past all that and
forgive me. Let's start over. Love you." I said and rolling
my eyes throwing my phone on the mattress. "Just all
bullshit like always." I added. "I'm glad you finally got rid
of her. She was no good." Sam said. "I know. I know." I

34

said. I could hear Gavin fighting with his little brother in the back ground. "You two knocked it off!" Sam yells. "Oh my god. I got to go girl before these two kill each other. But I will see you in a couple months!! Till then I'll text you in a bit!" She said with a huge smile. "Okay girl. Talk to you soon!" I said with a smile. "Love you! Bye! Sam said. "Love you too!" I said signing out of the chat.

Gracie cracks her neck. Her eyes are glossy as if she were holding back tears. She hits the power button on her computer so hard to where it is stuck in. "Shit.' She says to herself.

Moments after, there is a very rapid knocking at the front door. It startles me a bit as I sit for a minute thinking who it could be. Then it knocks again but louder. So I get up to answer the door. Upon approaching I see a car in the driveway. So I open the door aggravated because the knocking was honestly pissing me off. "What the hell are you doing here?" I said even more aggravated and a bit confused.

It was my ex Kristen who lives in Florida. She looked quite rough more than usual. Her hair was in a sloppy ponytail like it had not been washed in a few days and her pants had a couple of stains on it. The black circles under her eyes made her look like a raccoon. "Well don't look so happy to see me baby." She said as her smile went to a frown. "What do you want?" I asked. "Well since you haven't been answering my messages or calls I ..." as I interrupt her. "What. Thought you could drive eighteen hours to see me hoping that I would just take you in and forget everything that has happened? You must have lost

your damn mind." I said closing the door. "Wait!" Kristen
puts her hand on the door to stop it.

Gracie watches from her upstairs bedroom in anger
as she opens the window just enough to hear the
conversation better. "Listen, just hear me out and then if
you still want me to fuck off I will." Kristen pleaded.
"Have you been drinking?" I said knowing damn well she
was. I could smell it from where I was standing. She
ignored my question and replied "Please." She said "Well,
go on!" I said irritated. "I know I have hurt you. I have lied
and I am sorry. I really messed up. But I want to start over.
I'll stay here with you. We could start new and fresh."
Kristen said with tears in her eyes. "I appreciate the effort
you have made Kris, but I highly doubt you will ever get
that zipper fixed on your pants seeing it falls every time
you see a dick. Now leave me alone. Have a good life." I
said "And go sleep that alcohol off. You smell like a
fucking brewery." I added shutting the door. Kristen stood
at the porch for a few minutes staring at the door. She was
wobbling back and forth as she finally staggered her way
back to the car. I wait for her to leave.

As she walked to her car, Gracie watched with rage
growing inside of her. As Kristen left, Gracie slammed her
window shut making her way over to my house. She
knocked softly. "Seriously." I said to myself as I had just
started to unpack some of Jayce's things. I opened the door
abruptly thinking it was Kristen returning. "What!?" I said
rudely. "Is everything alright?" Gracie asked with a soft
voice. I run my hand over my eyes. "I'm so sorry. I didn't
know it was you." I said. "Yeah, everything is fine." I said

calming down taking a deep breath. "Would you like to go for a walk?" Gracie asked. "I'd love to." Sighing deeply closing the door behind me.

Gracie kept her sights on me from the corner of her eye. As I walked facing forward I was still a little upset from earlier. "So who was that girl if you don't mind me asking?" Gracie said with innocents. "How did you know there was anyone over?" I asked a little agitated. "I could hear yelling." Gracie replied innocently. "Just an ex-girlfriend." I said trying not to reveal too much about my past relationship. "Is she a bother?" Gracie asked. I chuckled a bit and replied "I guess you could say that." Gracie grinned staying silent.

We walked to a nice little creek that was along the path in the woods by Gracie's house. There were a few ducks floating by and the sound of crickets chirped. It was quite peaceful. We sat on this huge bolder that was on the edge of the creek. That water looked so clear I could see minnows swimming by. "I applied at the Cool Beans Café today." I said "Oh! That's such a cute little shop. I hope they call you!" Gracie said with excitement. "Me too. I really need something to do while Jayce is in school." I said with a chuckle. Gracie smiled and replied "You can hang out with me if you would like. I enjoy your company." She said touching my arm gently. I looked down at her hand smiling looking back to the creek. "This is really beautiful out here. Thank you for showing me." I said. "It's really no problem. I come out here a lot to clear my head sometimes." She says looking at the baby ducks walking with their momma alongside of us. "I'm glad we have such a cool neighbor like you. I was really worried moving here that we would have noisy or nosey neighbors. Which, back home, we had both, and it sucked." I added. "I'm glad I have someone to hang out with. I really like you guys." She said looking at me.

CHAPTER 5

Later the same evening, Kristen finds herself at a hole in the wall bar in Tenn. She is slamming back the scotch like it's water. Gracie sits in the parking lot waiting for Kristen to leave. Finally, two thirty a.m. rolls around. Kristen stumbles out of the bar; an older drunk gentleman helps her to the car. Kristen drives off as Gracie follows her a bit of way till they reach a long old bridge in the valley. Gracie gains speed and rides Kristen's bumper flashing her high beams causing Kristen to swerve all over the road. A semi passes Kristen beeping almost hitting her. Kristen grips the steering wheel and sits up in the seat. She starts to sweat and begins to panic. Kristen rubs her eyes thinking it would un-blur her drunken double vision. Gracie flashes her light uncontrollable till Kristen cannot see from the reflection in her rearview mirror blinding Kristen. She loses control of the wheel driving the car off the bridge into a huge lake.

Gracie proceeds to keep driving, pulling off down the road. She gets out of her car hiding behind some tall hedges to watch the car being submerged in water. The road seemed desolate, but Gracie kept her distance just in case.

Kristen tried desperately to break the window and open the door. But the pressure from the water kept the doors sealed shut. As for the window breaking, her impaired motor functions had made her too weak to even cause a chip. She sloppily kicks the window on the driver side more, grunting and crying at the same time. As the car hits the bottom of the lake, about fifteen feet down, Kristen sits trying to catch her breath listening to her car creek from the pressure of the water. The metal frame starts to make popping sounds startling Kristen. As water starts to flood the vents of the car and seeps through the car doors, the windows busts and floods with water. Gracie then gets back into her car and heads home.

Chapter 6

The following morning as I was getting ready to walk back home from dropping off Jayce, I get a phone call from the café. They wanted me to come in as soon as I could to start. I headed right over. I texted Gracie right before I went in to tell her they wanted me to come in. She replied that she was super happy for me. As I walked in, the smell of coffee beans bombarded my nostrils. Gracie was right it was a small yet cute café. Something I could definitely get used to. There were six booths and seven round high tops. Then a bar lined the back wall where the kitchen was. I approached the bar and asked for the manager. She came right out greeting me with a big smile and southern accent.

"You must be Nicole?" she said excitedly. She had the biggest green eyes I had ever seen. They reminded me of granny smith green apples. "In the flesh." I said jokingly. She chuckled "I am Donna." She shook my hand. "Nice to meet you Donna, you can call me Nick." I added "Well you are a cutie!" she said looking me up and down quickly. "Thank you Miss." I smiled. Donna was a confident young woman. The way she walked you could tell she was a woman in power here. Her hair was perfectly twisted into pigtails not one strand was misplaced. Her face looked so young as if she had never stressed a day in her life. Maybe early thirties just like Gracie. Both of them women you would never be able to tell they were a day past twenty. "Let me go make you a name tag. I'll be right back." She said. I took a look around the café at the pictures hanging on the walls. They were all in black and white with old cars and saloons in them. The owner of this place must be a big western culture fan. Donna runs back to me within minutes, handing me a black shirt with two beans on the back wearing sunglasses giving a thumbs up. It also had the name of the café in small print on the front *Cool Beans Café.* I went to the back to put it on.

After a couple of hours I was really getting the hang of it. I really was enjoying the people I was meeting till these two burly truck driver guys walked in. I seated them and asked what they would like. The one man replied. "A tall cup of you." He said winking. He was dirty looking with a long yellow and white beard. He had a torn up jean vest with holey jeans on. The once was white T-shirt underneath was a greasy dirty yellow color kind of the same color of his teeth. It reminded me of a brown paper bag from a Chinese restaurant that had grease spots everywhere. That really grossed me out. His southern drawl was really heavy too. It was almost hard to understand him. So to be polite I smiled and just repeated the question. "What can I get you fellas?" I asked again. His friend was as dirty as him and blew me a kiss. "I said I want a tall glass of you." He said more stern grabbed my leg. "Sir, please do not touch me." I said firmly. "Why, you don't like a man's' touch?" he said looking at his friend laughing.

His friend then chimed in "Clive, I don't think she likes that." As he laughed. "Looks like you dabble with the ladies. You one of them queers aren't you?" He added rudely. "Sir, I am going to have to ask you to leave if you do not cut it out." I said biting my cheek trying to keep my bad sailor mouth in check. "Or what? You gonna kick me out?" he said grabbing my wrist. I yanked my arm to my side instantly and walked to the back.

I took a moment to myself, while I watched them laugh and carry on from the kitchen. Crystal, one of my co-workers comes up beside me. "Are you okay?" she asked in a way when someone is just trying to act like they give a shit but really don't. "I am fine." I replied keeping my eyes on the men. "If you need something just holler." She said carrying to pots of coffee. My hands were a bit shaken from the frustration trying to get out from inside of me. I take a deep breath then proceed back to the table.

"Have you fellas decided?" I innocently asked. Then the tall trucker guy stood up getting in my face. "My tongue is just as good as any." He said sticking his tongue out and wiggling it. His breath smelled like onions and whiskey. He definitely skipped a few teeth brushings this week. "Let go of me." I said pulling my wrist back while trying to keep it low key.

I felt embarrassed, this was my first day. Already I had to deal with this. The crew that was working with me just watched in confusion as they waited their tables. I tried to step away but he grabbed my wrist tighter, so my instant response was to hit him as I did right in his eye. He didn't think twice, then he decked me with a right hook in my mouth. I went down knocking over the table behind me. I hear the gasps of the customers that were next to the table I just knocked over. Gracie runs in as if she knew I was in trouble, kneeling down to me "Someone get ice and a rag!" She yells to the other workers standing there watching the whole thing like it was a movie.

Then she looks up at the man who hit me. She stood up getting in his face. Mind you she isn't very tall maybe a strong 5'2 if I had to guess. So standing in front of this guy she looked so small but her words were so powerful in the sternness of her voice. As she says calmly "How's the coffee? Hot I hope." As she takes a pot full of coffee still steaming on the counter next to her and throws it in his eyes. He held his hands over his face as he yelled in pain. "You bitch!" he yelled. The friend of the man took off like a coward. Gracie grabbed the man buy the shirt and pulled him close to her face. As she whispered to him "I would leave town if I were you." as she pushed the man away from her, he stumbled out the door.

Gracie kneeled back down to me "Are you okay?" she asked keeping my head elevated. "Yeah" I said wiping my lip as I was bleeding pretty well. Crystal came from the back with a rag with some ice in it. As Grace grabs it and holds it to the side of my mouth. "Took you long enough. Did you have to crochet the rag?" Gracie said aggravated to the Crystal. "Come on. You are done for the day." She said helping me up and to the car. The whole place was quiet and stunned by what had just taken place.

I stayed quiet for the first five minutes of the ride. "Thank you." I said a little embarrassed from all that just happened. "That guy was so disrespectful." She said with agitation in her voice. "Yeah, well I've dealt with it most of my life. It's okay." I said "NO!" she said loudly. I looked at her startled. It echoed off the windows in the car. I haven't seen her angry yet. "No it's not." She added toning her

44

voice down. I just continued to look forward because the way she was so irritated had me a little nervous.

We pulled into her driveway sitting in the car for a couple of minutes in silence. "Please, let me take care of that for you." She said caressing my cheek. I took a deep breath, nodding my head yes. I walked into her house and sat on the couch holding the rag to my busted lip still. The cat came running in sniffing my feet purring.

She brought in a fresh washcloth with a bowl of warm water and some more ice. "He likes you." She said with a smirk. She sat on the couch close to me wiping the dried blood from my cheek, lips and chin. As she gazed at me maintaining a grin, I tried not to make a lot of eye contact but I could see her staring at me as I looked at the cat. She softly patted my bloody lip to get all the dry blood off of it. She then softly pressed a fresh ice cloth back on my lip. "Oww." I whispered under my breath. "I'm sorry." She said softly. My lip was very tender, I have only been hit in the eye before but that was in second grade by this kid named Trudy. He took my notebook so I stomped on his foot and he popped me in the eye.

She turned my head to face her as she moved my hair off my sweaty forehead. She kept a smile on her face as she stared at me with those big brown eyes. I was sweating from all the adrenaline. I felt greasy I needed a shower. I looked down at my lap and took the ice off my lip for a minute. It was making my face numb from the coldness and quite frankly it was starting to burn like frost bite. I felt my lip starting to bleed again. Gracie lifted my chin up with her index finger leaning in to kiss me softly. It was so warm and loving. I could feel my blood smearing between our lips like it was lip gloss. I had my eyes open for a moment as I wasn't too sure as to what was going on but then I closed them seeing she had hers closed. I started feeling something I never felt before. It wasn't like anything I have ever experienced in a kiss. Her tongue tasted like vanilla chocolate and a hint of mint. As if she was eating vanilla chocolate beforehand then chewed gum after. I could taste my blood a smidge too. You know that metallic taste you get when you bit your tongue or something. So I know she did as well. Our lips fit perfectly together. Her kiss felt like a rose petal pressing on my tender busted lip. She was so gentle with her tongue massaging mine that it could have put me to sleep. She wasn't a sloppy kisser but I think I had an idea that she wasn't judging from the way everything in her house was so neat and perfect.

Her left hand cradled the right side of my jaw bone. It was so soft like she moisturized at least twenty times a day. Her hand felt like a velvet blanket against my cheek I felt so chill. I could smell the lavender lotion too. Her right hand rested on my left knee so still not even a tremble. In this moment I could feel she had this strong connection to me. It was as if she was deeply in love. Like I was the only person in her world. But how could that be? We have only known each other for a short time. As I looked at her pulling away I notice a little bit of my blood laced on her bottom lip. "Oh..uhm." I said as I went to wipe it off, as she smiled and licked her lip slowly as to not leave any blood behind. Like it was a cherished reminisces of her favorite flavor. It weird me out at first but then I thought about it and it kind of was a turn on but I made no comment I just smiled.

She had an old grandfather clock in the room we were in as the bell rang two times; I realized I would be late to pick up Jayce. "Shit." I said softly. "What's wrong?" she said concerned. "I have to go get Jayce. But I'm not going to make it in time." I said getting up off the couch walking to the door. "Well I will take you." She said grabbing her keys. "Are you sure?? You have done so much already for me." I said "Non sense. I want to help." She said touching my arm and opening the door walking us out.

CHAPTER 7

Kendyle sits in his office, noticing the news is on in the other room that he can see from across the way. As it peaks his interests, he makes his way closer the TV in the main lobby. As the news explains the event. "A young woman from Key West Florida, Kristen Ann Bell twenty seven, was found dead in the River Bend Lake this morning by two fishermen. Police say the car may have lost control and gone over the bridge trapping the young woman inside. An autopsy will determine if alcohol was a factor." The news reporter said.

One of the men Kendyle works with comes to stand beside him. "Damn drunk drivers huh?" The man says. "I think I know her." Kendyle replies. "Ex-girlfriend?" the man asks. "Yeah, well my sisters ex-girlfriend. But I didn't know she was even here." Kendyle says confused. "Love makes us do stupid shit sometimes." The man says. "I'm Calvin Davis by the way. I'm down the hall from you." He added. "Kendyle Shaw." Kendyle says shaking Calvin's hand. He was a short husky guy with silver glasses and hair the color of snow. Kendyle had to look down at him he was so short. "Kendyle? Yeah I heard about you." Calvin says. "Really? Good things I hope." Kendyle says with a grin. "Oh yeah yeah! Just that you are a transfer from Florida and your wife is in the military that's about all I really know." Calvin says with a chuckle. "Well I better get back. I got to be in the court at two thirty. Good to meet you. We will have to do lunch or something to get to know one another." Calvin smiles and proceeds to the elevator.

"Yeah, will do." Kendyle replies walking back to his office still puzzled.

Kendyle arrives home later that day and walks into the house with the intention to ask Nicole why she didn't tell him Kristen came. He walks into the living room as Jayce, Gracie and I sit on the floor playing Uno. "Hey brother, how was work?" I ask. "It was alright" as Kendyle walks over to Jayce kissing the top of his head. "Hey buddy. Hi Gracie how are you?" He asks crouching down to our level. "I'm great!" she replied. Kendyle then looks at me ".... Can I talk to you for a minute?" Kendyle asks. "Yeah, of course." I said getting up from the floor following him to the kitchen which is the next room over. "What's up?" I said putting my hands in my back pockets. "Umm..." as he looks at my lip. " What happened??" he said. "It's a long story. I'll tell you later." I said shrugging it off. "Are you okay?" he asked "Yeah, Gracie took care of me. It's all good. "I said with a big grin. "Yeah, about that. Are you burning the candle at both ends?" he asked with his one eye brow raised.

Meanwhile, Gracie keeps her focus on our conversation while still playing with Jayce. "What the hell are you talking about?" I said a little agitated. "Was Kristen here?" he asked firmly. "She stopped by yesterday but I had no idea she was going to do that. I mean that's psycho shit for real." I said "How did you know?" I asked. "Well, I saw on the news today that she drove her car into the Lake and drown." He said in a sincere voice as he didn't know how I would take it. "What?" I asked in disbelief. Gracie develops a vile smile. Kendyle pulls his phone out and brings it up on the internet. "Look." He said showing me the article.

I take the phone as my stomach dropped. I guess I felt a little guilty for letting her drive while knowing she was intoxicated. On the other hand it honestly wasn't my fault. I mean, she had been driving like that for who knows how many hours before she even got to my house. "She was drunk when she got here." I said. "Well what did she want?" he asked. "What do you think? To work things out." I answered. "And what did you tell her?" Kendyle asked in a stern voice. "Let's runaway and get married." I said sarcastically. Kendyle crossed his arms. "I told her no fucking way. What did you think I would tell her?" I said irritated. "Well, I know what kind of affect she has had on you in the past; I was just making sure my baby sister learned her lesson after five times of trying that's all." Kendyle looked at me then let it go. "I'm sorry sis; I don't mean to give you a hard time. I was just letting you know. It seems you have had a rough day. I wasn't trying to add to it." He said pulling me in for a hug. "It's okay. I know you are just being the big brother. I promised you I wouldn't fall for her shit again and I meant it." I said embracing him back. "I know, I just cannot see you go through that again. I love you." He said kissing my cheek.

We play Uno for a bit more till Jayce has to go to bed. "Alright bud time for bed." I said. "Can you read me a story auntie Nicki?" Jayce said with his sea blue eyes. "Certainly! But go brush your teeth first. I'm going to walk Gracie home." I said. "Okay! Bye Gracie!" Jayce said as he gave her a big hug then ran to the bathroom. "Bye sweetie."

Gracie replied. "Thanks for hanging out with us Gracie." Kendyle said walking us to the door. "Thank you for letting me stay. I really had a great evening." She added.

I walked Gracie to her porch. As we stood by the door she turned to look at me with those honey brown eyes. "Thank you so much for everything today. You have been a great neighbor." I said "You are an amazing person Nicole Shaw." Gracie said stepping closer to me. Kendyle watched us from the living room window discretely. "You are going to make me blush Miss Lovely." I said smiling ear to ear. "Is that a bad thing?" she asked. "No, it's just been awhile." I said. "And what did I say about calling me Miss?" she said jokingly stepping nose width away from my face with a big smile. "That you love it." I said laughing nervously.

She smiled and gave me another kiss on the lips so soft that it tickled my bottom lip. "Goodnight." She whispered slipping into the darkness of the house. "Goodnight" I said as I started my way back home. Kendyle ran to the other room like he wasn't watching. I read Jayce a story as he effortlessly fell asleep on my side. I got up as slow and quite as I could, covering him up, kissing his forehead.

As I walk quietly down the hall Kendyle whispers from his bedroom. "Hey" "What" I whisper back walking into his room. "So...you hitting' that?" he chuckled talking about Gracie. "Get out of here. Were you watching you ease dropper?" I said walking over to his bed. "I was being nosey yes." He giggled. "Well for your information she kissed me." I said in a funny voice. "Mmmhmm." Kendyle said in disbelief. "I am for real punk." I said taking his pillow and hitting him with it. He laughed "I'm going to bed." I said as Kendyle continued to laugh. "Sweet dreams." Kendyle said in a funny voice. "Don't hate." I whispered back.

I lay down on my mattress closing my eyes. My phone beeped so I picked it up. It was a picture from Gracie. I waited in anticipation as it downloaded. It was her in bed in just panties and her arm over her breasts with a mischievous grin. I stared like I was put under a spell. I felt my body get hot starting to sweat. I could feel a trickle of perspiration run down the small of my back. So I texted her "You're beautiful." With a winking emoji at the end. I put my phone on my chest as I anxiously awaited her reply back. She was real quick with the response and I mean like seconds quick. "Thank you. Where is mine?" she texted. "I'm a bit shy." I texted back. "Maybe after you are more acquainted with me." She texted back with a smiling emoji. "Definitely" I texted back. "Goodnight sweetheart." She texted "Goodnight beautiful." I replied as I dozed off to sleep.

A few hours pass, at three am I hear a car drive down the road and pull into Gracie's driveway. I am out of it a bit thinking nothing of it, falling back asleep. After I walked Gracie home, she waited till the wee hours of the night to leave. She found the two men that harassed me earlier that day. They were staying at a rundown motel just down the road from the café I worked at. She put on a pair of black gloves as she riffled through the one mans' semi-truck. She found that he was a bit of a heroin junkie. She pulled his stash out and proceeded to find his room. She was dressed slutty with a high black tight skirt on black high heels and a very low cut top that barely covered her torso. She walked into the front office and faked a southern drawl. "Excuse me sir, I'm meeting me husband here, he drives that big red truck out there. I think he may have fallen asleep on me before giving me the room number." As she fake laughs. "Could you be so kind as to giving me that room number." She added as she bent over the counter pushing her tits up with her arms as she leaned showing all cleavage. The clerk couldn't help but to stare at her breasts. She knew how to manipulate a person into doing anything. "Yes ma'am he is in room 109." He said with a real southern drawl handing her the extra key. Not one second did he take his eyes off her breasts. His hands trembled as she grabbed the key from him brushing her fingers on the top of his hand. "You are a doll." She said winking and walking out.

She took a look around as she put back on the gloves and let herself in. She closed the door behind her leaving the lights off. The man was in a very deep sleep. His snoring could tear down a wall or two. It rumbled the ground a bit and it sounded like he was choking almost. The room had a foul odor of mildew, sweaty feet, and alcohol. Grace proceeded to the side of the mans' bed standing there in silence watching him breathe. Gracie had seven full syringes in her hands raising them getting ready to impale this man. She used all her strength striking him with the syringes, injecting him with them at the same time in his throat. The man popped up and was discombobulated. "What the fuck. Who are you??" he said very slurred. He held his throat and gasped for air. He tried grabbing Gracie's face but the drug soon took over his motor functions making him very unable to do anything. Gracie said softly "I told you to leave town." Gracie watched the man crawl on the floor holding his arm out. He choked on his bloody spit leaking it all over the old stained carpet. Gracie walked herself out locking the door behind her. She gets into her car she parked down the road and puts the gloves into a plastic bag. She rides to a nearby dumpster tossing the bag in it to rid the evidence.

When I arrive at the café the next day, I notice yellow caution tape swinging in the breeze at a hotel across the way. Then as I approach the door of the café I could see a bunch of cops and reporters down the street. "What is going on?" I ask Donna. "They don't know yet" she replied. I see a body being taking out on a stretcher with a white sheet placed over it. Donna grabbed my arm. "Are you okay?" she asked as I was just staring emotionless at the body. "Yeah, I am fine." I said turning to face Donna. I gave her a smile then looked back at the hotel parking lot. I see the same semi-truck that I saw yesterday sitting in the parking lot of the hotel. Then I thought to myself that things were starting to get strange. It seemed as if I had a problem with someone the next day something happens to them. Then fear set in shortly after. Am I a suspect? I am the last person to come into contact with Kristen and now this trucker guy.

I text my brother about what I saw. I was getting more nervous the more I thought about it. "Dyle, am I a suspect if I am the last person to see someone alive?" I texted him. He responded quickly after. "It really depends.

Why what is going on?" he texted. "I will have to explain later in person." I texted him back. Not that his answer relieved my stress any but I haven't been acting suspicious so I should be okay.

I receive a phone call from Jayce's' school about an hour later. The principle told me I was to come there immediately. "Donna, I'm sorry I have an emergency. I have to go!" I exclaimed. "Okay!" she said worried. So I left running to the school thinking something bad happened to Jayce. I find the office twenty minutes later. This school was really huge. It was more like a college campus. It had three buildings and a directory buy the library that sat nearby. I walk into the office where I see Jayce sitting with his head down at the principles desk. "Hey" I said softly to him crouching down in front of him where he was sitting. I caressed is face and felt the moistness of his cheeks from tracks of tears.

The principle comes walking in. "Ms. Shaw?" he asked. I stood up to shake his hand. "Yes." I replied. "Please have a seat." He said. I sat next to Jayce putting my hand on his back gently rubbing it. "Are you his mom?" he asked. "No, I am his aunt. His mom is overseas right now." I said. "And the father?" he said in a monotone voice not looking at me once. His face was buried in a yellow folder that had Jayce's name on it. "My brother, he is at work. I take care of Jayce primarily. I'm sorry but what's going on?" I said confused. "Jayce is a good kid. But he seems to have found trouble with one of the boys here." He said. "Trouble? How?" I asked looking at Jayce. He remained to keep his head down. "There is an older boy Red that I often times catch with Jayce doing things they shouldn't. Today I found them in the bathroom while they were writing all over the walls with permeant marker." He said. "He gave me a wedgie and it hurt. Then I cried and he made fun of me. He said if I didn't write on the walls he was going to beat me up." Jayce said starting to cry again. I grabbed him holding him tight. "How long has this been going on??" I said aggravated. "I am not sure." He replied. "Jayce, how long bud?" I grabbed Jayce's face to make him look at me in a gentle way. "Since I got here." He said hesitantly. "Why didn't you tell me?" I asked. "Because I want to be a big boy for you aunt Nicki." He said grabbing me for a hug again. "Awe buddy! You are a big boy." I said feeling overwhelmed by this.

I felt so angry with this kid Red that I wanted to hurt him, but I knew I couldn't. "Ms. Shaw, sometimes these things escalate to higher activity and sometimes the bullied act back but very worse. I just do not want to see any revenge." The principle said. "Revenge. Seriously. You really think a seven year old boy knows anything about revenge?" I asked angrily. "I am just saying. Especially when children his age that do not have stable parents around. They tend to act out." He replied. "Excuse me, but his parents are stable. They both work demanding jobs. And I am a stable guardian." I said agitated. "Have you apprehended this Red kid??" I added angrily. "Not yet. His parents are hard to get ahold of." He replied with hesitation. "Well give me the fucking address I'll go there myself." I said pissed. "This is what I mean." He said. "Excuse me?" I said getting more aggravated. "The revenge will come from the people raising these boys. " He said. I stood up with

Jayce picking him up to carry him. "In all sincerity Mr. Lang. Go fuck yourself." I said as a slammed the office door.

Jayce being bullied by this kid Red really set me off. He was in sixth grade and so much bigger than all the other kids. I was so angry that later on that evening after my brother came home, I went to Gracie's to vent to her. "It really pisses me off! I want to strangle this damn kid." I said frustrated. "Even though Jayce is my nephew, he is still like my son!" I added.

She comes walking into the living room from the kitchen wearing a grey long button up sweater and black booty short. She handed me a cup of hot coco. "Here drink this. It will help you calm down." She said with a big smile as she sat on the couch closely next to me putting one of her legs on my lap and the other was crossed under her. I took a sip of the coco. "Wow. That's delicious." I said calming down. "It's homemade." She replied smiling taking a sip of her tea. "Do you put anything special in it?" I asked. She shook her head yes maintaining a smile. "Oh, it's a secret?" I asked smiling. She nodded yes smiling bigger showing her beautiful white straight teeth.

She set her cup down on the glass table in front of us and put her arm around my neck. "Don't worry about this Red kid. I will start taking you two, to and from the school. And if he gives Jayce a problem, I will help you take care of it." She said kissing my cheek. I smiled and said "Okay." She kissed my lips then ran her fingers through my hair. "You look tired." She said softly still playing with the front of my hair. "Yeah, I am now. I don't

57

know why. It just all of a sudden hit me." I said finishing my coco. "You can rest here if you like. I don't mind." She said laying my head on the back of the couch as she played with my hair. The last thing I remember was looking at her as I dozed off.

The early morning sun crept into the window of Gracie's bedroom. I heard her get up slowly. I felt her softly kiss me on the lips. Then I hear her turning on the shower. I was slightly discombobulated as I do not remember coming up here last night. I turned to look at her side of the bed, upon her bleach white pillow laid a bright red rose that was on the verge of bloom. It made me smile as I inhaled the scent from it.

The fresh rose made me realize that I was not that fresh since I forgot my toothbrush so I sifted through her drawer next to her side of the bed. I was hoping to find gum or mints, or a possible piece of chocolate. I found a prescription bottle with two round white pills in it as I read the label *Haloperidol Initial dose: 0.5 to 5 mg orally 2 to 3 times a day. Maintenance dose: 1 to 30 mg/day in 2 to 3 divided doses. Do not exceed 100mg in one day.* I had no idea what it was for.

Gracie stands in her doorway silent with the towel around her. "I was going to tell you." She says after watching me read the label. "Oh...umm." I stuttered nervously startled putting it back and shutting the drawer. She walked over to the bed sitting next to me. "I...I was looking for some gum or something... I forgot my toothbrush." I said nervously. She pets the back of my head. "It's ok." As she giggled. "I'm not ashamed. I just didn't know how to tell you. I certainly do not want to scare you off." She said looking deep into my eyes. "That doesn't scare me. Some people need that stuff. I'm not judging." I said feeling a little better. I still had no clue what it was used for. I didn't want to ask since I wanted to make it seem like I knew what it was. She smiled and put her hand on my back "Perfect." She said.

Chapter 8

Red rode his bike to school. He had red curly hair and looked like he was always missing a shower. Chubby kid with freckles and a dirty T-shirt that looked as if he fell into a mud pit. One day after school, Red sees Jayce walking out to Gracie's car with me in the passenger seat. Red runs up to Jayce "Hey you bitch!" as he snatches Jayce's backpack off of him. Gracie and I quickly get out of the car running over to them. "What do you think you're doing?" I say as I hold Jayce close to me. "Whatever the hell I want bitch." He replied in a vulgar tone. Gracie grabs the backpack from Red giving him an evil glare the entire time. "Hasn't your mother taught you any manners?" Gracie says in a stern low voice.

Red freezes while he stares at Gracie. I saw him clench his fist with a tremble. For a moment it seemed like he was going to throw a punch but something stopped him. I could see the fear in Red's eyes, almost tearing up. I swear they were having a staring contest. I could feel in the pit of my stomach like something was about to go down. "Gracie." I said to snap her out of it. I see her smirk in a demented manner. She doesn't look at me just keeps her eyes on the ill-mannered boy.

Gracie bends slightly down to this kid's height as she didn't have to go far. Red was about her height, for his age he was huge. "Listen, I do not play games. I suggest you apologize to my friend Jayce." She says in a soft but yet stern voice yet again. Red steps closer to Gracie almost touching noses "Or what?" He said in a mean low tone as his eyes filled with rage. Gracie did a little giggle under her

60

breath as she stood up. "Do not test me." She replied as she crossed her arms gritting her teeth together. "Come on Gracie. They are just being stupid kids." I said as Jayce and I walked back to the car. Gracie stood still not taking her eyes off Red. "I'll see you tomorrow cupcake." The kid yelled at Jayce. "And I got your stupid kid right here bitch." He added yelling at me grabbing his crotch. Gracie shook her head. "Are you done?" She asked. "For today." He said laughing walking away with his two little buddies.

Gracie watched them walk over to the bike rack then proceeded to the car. "Jayce, don't let that kid bully you okay?" I said. Jayce kept his head down and shook it yes. "Buddy, it's not your fault, some kids are just stupid." I added as Gracie got in the car exhaling deeply. She looked in the back seat at Jayce. "Do those kids always bother you honey?" she said. He kept his head down with a mumbled tone "Yes." Gracie looks at me with a smile. "Well if they bother you again you tell us okay?" she says patting his knee. Gracie turns back around kissing me on the cheek. The next day I let Jayce stay home. I spent the day with him.

In the evening Gracie sits down the road from the school waiting to watch Red leave. She follows behind him a good distance to not cause a scene. A gentle mountain mist starts to drizzle in the Tennessee air. Red lives on a dirt road out in the country side. The dirt was slippery from the drizzle and he gets a little nervous with a vehicle following. He keeps peering over his shoulder as he starts to pedal faster. The bike tires start to slip making it difficult to catch traction.

61

Gracie speeds up to make him more nervous to where she is practically riding his back wheel. Red is out of breath, getting tired and sweaty. There is a narrow bridge coming up. It can barely fit one car on it. Below are crumbled tunnels that at one point use to be a river. Now it is just a lot of jagged rocks. Gracie bumps his back tire as they get on the bridge. Red loses control of his bike; it goes downhill towards the crumble. He tries to put on the breaks but they will not work. He hits a big bump flying over his handlebars off his bike. He lands into the crumble being impaled through the middle of his chest with a long sharp tree branch that was sticking out of the rocks down below. Gracie gets out of her car and glairs at Red. He shakes uncontrollably touching the branch sticking out of his chest. He uses the effort he has left to turn his head to face Gracie as he is gasping for his last breaths. She pulls her shades down to her nose as she says. "This is what I'm doing about it." As she slides them back up and gets in the car to leave, not looking back.

Kendyle came home early. The three of us decide to enjoy the beautiful weather and play a little football outside. It was just the right temperature after the rain. The sun came out shinning so brightly. Gracie watches me from her living room window discretely. As she is watching me, she traces her lips down to the middle of her chest with her fingertips. She sees almost as if I were playing in slow motion. She bits her bottom lip as if I were seducing her. She sees the sweat on my shirt and the sun glistening of my wet skin. She runs her fingers down her body to her vagina as she softly touches herself. She closes her eyes drowning out everyone but my voice. A few moments later she walks outside and sits on her porch. I glance to see Gracie sitting there with her hands folded smiling with a dark purple sweater and black shades. "Hey!" I yelled. "Hey! What's the score?" Gracie replied. "You know I'm kicking these boys' asses!" I said with a chuckle. Kendyle grabs the ball from my hand and runs with it. "Yeah, you are really kicking ass when you are distracted." Kendyle said. "Wanna play?" I said. "I like to watch. I'm not much of a sports chick." Gracie said. "Let's give the gal a show." Kendyle said with a smirk.

After an hour of playing around with the boys, I had to go into the café for a few hours. "Someone called off today so I said I would cover." I said to Kendyle. "Okay sis, you want me to take you?" he asked as Gracie came walking over. "I'll take her so you can play with Jayce more." She said innocently. "Yeah, that would be better bro. You don't get to see him often." I said as I kissed Jayce on the head. "Kick daddy's booty bud." I said to Jayce. "OHH I will!" he said grabbing the ball from Kendyle as he chased him around in the yard.

Gracie dropped me off at work. "I can pick you up if you would like." She said smiling at me. "Okay, that sounds good. I get off at nine." I said. She leaned over to kiss me. "Have a good shift." She said. I smiled and walked in. She watched me as Donna came over to greet me. "Thank you for coming in." she said putting her hand on my shoulder. "No problem." I said. Gracie gripped her steering wheel leaving indents in the rubber. She gritted her teeth together to where her jaw bone even made a cracking sound. I felt eyes on me as I glanced over my shoulder.

Gracie was still sitting in the parking lot watching me. I waved at her in a confused way. I didn't know why she was still sitting there. She waved back with a big forced smile. As she pulled out of the parking lot skidding the rocks. I just shrugged it off.

Donna hands me an orange flyer. "I am having a Halloween party. I would really like it if you came." She said giving me a big smile. "Sweet! I'll be there. I love Halloween." I said. "Perfect! You can dress up if you want." She replied. "Alright. I will definitely find a cool costume to wear then." I said smiling at her. "What are you gonna be?" I asked "I haven't decided yet, but I'm really leaning towards Carrie, the blood scene!" she said with excitement. "That sounds pretty rad. Blood and all huh?" I said with a chuckle. "Hell yeah girl, that's the best!" she said winking at me walking to the back. I folded the flyer and put it in my back pocket.

Gracie picks me up right on time. I get in the car and she gives me a big kiss as Donna walks out of the café locking up. Donna looks right as Gracie kisses me. Gracie glares at Donna while she does so. "How was work?" she asked excited to see me. I smile because she made me feel so wanted. "It was busy which made time fly." I said smiling at her. Donna looks back down as Gracie looks at her. I'm not paying any attention to what was taking place. I am kind of oblivious sometimes.

Later on that evening Gracie walks over to my house. She taps lightly on the door. "I'll get it." I say to the boys. "Hey Gracie, what's up?" I said happily. "Umm I was wondering if you could come help me with my hot tub.

I just got the damn thing a few months ago and haven't used it yet. It's all high tech; I'm not too good with things like that. As you know." She said a little embarrassed. "Yeah sure I'll come take a look." I said. "Dyle, I'll be back in a few. I'm going to Gracie's" I yelled to my brother. "Okay sis." He yelled back.

We walked to her back yard. It was so beautiful full of yellow and while lilies. I could see the greenhouse off in the distance by the wood line. The dark wood deck that was attached to the house looked as if it was just done. The dark cedar wood looked untouched by the elements. I could even smell the fresh cut cedar dust. At the top of the three stairs leading up to the deck was a wooden garden arbor with grapes vines wrapped decoratively around it with white lights intertwined.

As you walk onto the deck to the left is the hot tub made out of cherry oak. Its deep red color reminded me of velvet cake. "Well here it is." She said walking me over to it. "Wow. It's really nice." I said smiling at Gracie. I looked at the controls. It all looked quite simple. I think she was just trying to find ways to get me over here. "I tried turning it on, but no avail." She said with a giggle. I smiled and said "You may need to reset the breaker for it." Her desert brown eyes shined in the moonlight it was hard not to stare. "I never even thought of that." She said walking over to the little grey box mounted on the porch banister. She reset the breaker and I turned it on. "Tudaa" I said holding my arms out like I was a magician cracking a corky smile. "And look..." as I pressed another button. "We have bubbles." I said. "I love bubbles." She replied as she walked behind me running her hand on the small of my back. "Would you like to stay for a while and keep me company?" she asked innocently. I paused for a moment so I wouldn't sound too desperate with my answer. "Sure." I said softly. "Perfect. Would you like a glass of wine?" she asked. "I'll give it a try." I said as she passed behind me again walking into her house through the sliding glass doors. "I'll be right back." She added with seduction.

I stood there nervous with a pain in my stomach and a quiver in my knees. My palms began to get clammy so I kept wiping them on my shorts. She came back out handing me a glass of wine. I didn't drink alcohol but I didn't want to be rude. I noticed she put on a black laced robe also. It flowed effortlessly in the gentle night breeze.

I sat at the cedar bench placed next to the hot tub. She sat next to me looking up at the sky. "It is such a beautiful night." She said sipping her wine slowly. The way her lips kissed the rim of the wine glass gave me chills. She stood up taking off her black lace robe she had put on before she came back outside. Her bathing suit was all black lace as well. The bra pushed her breasts up high and close to where the perfect V shape was carved in her chest. The cheekini bottoms hugged her hips as the bottom of her ass cheeks were exposed. It looked like to perfectly round cherries next to one another. She stood on the step to get into the tub. She took the hair tie that was around her wrist to put her long dark brown hair into a perfect bun.

As she stepped into the tub she looked at me and smiled. "Care to join me?" she gave a vixen smirk. "I...I have nothing to wear." I said with a nervous chuckle. "We are both ladies, you can go nude." She said getting in the water, sitting down sipping on her wine. "How about my panties and bra? Will that do?" I said. "Whatever makes you comfortable honey." She said never taking her eyes off me once. I hesitantly got up wiping my hands one last time on my shorts discretely. I took my shoes, socks, and shorts off. "Oooo.. It's a bit chilly." I said talking about the deck. The mid October air was a bit chilled. "It's getting hot over here." She said brushing her fingertips across her chest. I nervously chuckled "I guess that's why they call it a hot tub." I said in a humorous manner, trying to rid this knot in my stomach.

I slowly climbed into the tub. "Are you going to leave your shirt on?" she asked. "I'm a little self-conscious." I said. Which, I never understood about myself because I'm fit, I just never thought of myself as pretty I guess. "Don't be ridiculous. You are gorgeous." She said with a serious tone. I nervously took my shirt off and sat next to Gracie. "Do you like the wine?" she asked. "Umm yeah it's alright." I said reaching to grab the glass from the arm of the bench. I took a sip and set it back down.

I kept my head turned for a minute as my lips puckered from the sour wine taste that I wasn't used to. "I really like your personality. I think that's what draws me to you." Gracie said scooting closer to me. "Oh yeah? My brother thinks I'm a smart ass. I tell him I learn from the best." I said grinning but not looking at her. "No. You're different." She said moving in front of me to look me in the eyes. "I see pain behind those beautiful blue eyes." She said as she traced her fingertips on my hairline down to my jaw bone. "Pain that I can take away." She added as she sat on my lap facing me. I froze at this point as I didn't know really what to do.

She was so sweet and hypnotizing she was making me fall for her without even trying. The T lights hanging from the open porch roof made her eyes stand out even more glistening like the sun on the ocean. That deep rich brown color almost looked black in the night sky but it was illuminating and captivating. She put her arms around my neck slowly leaning in to kiss me. I could taste the wine on her lips it made my mouth water. I put my hands on her hips and scooted her closer to me. I moved my hands up on her back unhooking her bra taking it off one strap at a time. She smiled with a little giggle biting her bottom lip with seduction. She gazed into my eyes as she put her fingers slowly through my hair. I picked her up and sat her on the edge of the tub while I kissed her neck. She ran her hands down my back grabbing my ass pushing me in between her legs. She closed her eyes putting her head back in euphoria.

I took her panties off, kissing my way down to her vagina. She put her legs over my shoulders as I cradle her body in my arms. I could taste the salt from her vaginal walls fill my mouth with a hint of the chlorine from the water. She grabbed the back of my head pushing me in deeper. Her moans were music to my ears. The way she said my name it was like out of a perfect love scene. She gripped the wooden banister that lined the back of the hot tub. She reached her climax almost instantly but she didn't want me to stop so I kept going. The louder she got I thought she was going to wake the neighbors that lived about a block away. "Should we take this inside?" I said. "Let them listen and be jealous." She said looking into my eyes pulling me up to her. She pulled my head towards her as she went in for an aggressive kiss.

It almost made me lose my grip on her but I sat back down putting her back onto my lap. She continued to kiss me. "I have wanted you since the first time I laid eyes on you." She said out of breath. "Really?" I said kissing her neck. "Fuck yeah." She replied grabbing my chin kissing my mouth more. She took my hand and pushed it down between her legs. I gently massaged her clitoris with my fingers. She rocked back and forth till she climaxed again.

She slowed down her movement till she came to a stop. Then she pried her lips off mine staring and smiled at me. She slowly got close to my ear whispering "I love you." Then looked back at me. I was a bit stunned at the moment as everything kind of happened so fast I needed a moment to think. "I love you too." I replied. I meant it, I just felt as if it was all happening quick but maybe not. I mean, people get married after two weeks of knowing each other now days for Christ sakes. I guess it was okay to say I love you to her.

We have known each other a little more than a month now. Her smile was so big like a kid in a candy shop. She gently kissed my lips again. "Will you stay the night with me?" she asked softly. "Yeah, of course." I said smiling back. "But, I have to be up early to get Jayce ready." I added. "No worries, I wouldn't let you forget that." She said as she kissed me again then got out of the hot tub. Her naked body was dripping that hot water. The

69

steam coming off of her from the cold air meeting her hot body was killing me. It looked like the steam coming off hot pavement after a downpour of rain on a summer's day. "See you inside." She winked and walked inside. I sat there for a moment trying to take everything in catching a thought. I think I held my breath most of the time. I was so damn nervous. I took a deep breath getting out walking to the door. She handed me a towel as I walked in. "OOH!" I said loudly. "You scared me." I said softly. "I'm sorry baby. I didn't mean to." She said from the darkness of the dining room where the sliding door was.

I dried off walking to the living room where she was making a fire in the fire place. "I thought we could keep this beautiful evening going by laying here by the fire." She said. "Sounds good to me." I replied putting my shirt on. I took of my wet bra and panties. Gracie laid there naked. I lay next to her. "You don't have to keep your shirt on silly." she said putting her hand on my chest. I smiled sitting up to take it off. "You're so beautiful." She whispered looking at my naked body. I lay back down as she laid her head on my chest with her arm around me. I felt her put one leg on mine. They were so soft like she had just shaved them. Her skin was a bit chilled from the water drying. The warmth from her vagina kept my right thigh warm. I held her through the night listening to her breathe as I looked at the ceiling. I laid my head against hers and finally fell asleep.

Gracie gets up before me without even disturbing me sleeping. She walks over to my clothes lying on the ground. Gracie folds my clothes neatly and puts them on the table next to us. She sees something in the back pocket of my shorts. She takes out the flyer I had folded earlier yesterday and reads it. She glares at me for a moment getting a bit angry. She memorizes the address along with the date then puts it back into my shorts proceeding to the kitchen.

I opened my eyes; I was confused as to where I was at for a moment. I was facing a stone fireplace that was still burning slightly like it had been all night. The feel of a velvet blanket covered me. It was so soft and warm. I rolled over on my back. The sun warmed my face from the window straight ahead of me. After awaking a couple minutes I realized I was still at Gracie's'. She walked into the living room with a TV tray in her hands. "Well good morning sleepy head." Gracie said kneeling down to me. I sat up to look at what she brought in.

The two sunny side eggs were perfectly round like she had cookie cut them. The toast was a golden brown and the orange juice smelled so fresh you would think she went outside to pick the orange from a tree. A fresh red rose rested between the plates, I picked it up to smell it. "Looks fresh." I said with a smile. "It is." She smiled back. "This looks great. Thank you." I said taking the tray. "Nothing for you?" I said biting the toast. "I'm making tea." She said with a smile. The bell went off on the grandfather clock as I realized it was Friday and Jayce needed to get to school. I was so late. "Shit!" I said as I set the tray on the floor and got up. "What's wrong??" Gracie asked in a worried tone. "I have to take Jayce to school! And he is alone in the house right now!" I said looking for my clothes. Gracie got

71

up gently grabbing my arm. "Hey. I took him. Everything is okay." She said calmly. I stopped abruptly looking at Gracie confused. "You did?" I asked. "Yeah. I didn't want to wake you. You looked so at peace." She said. "How…how did that work?" I asked still confused. "I went over there silly." she said with a soft chuckle. "Now just sit and eat the rest of your breakfast before it gets cold." She said walking me back to the tray.

I finished my food then looked at Gracie. "Thank you for breakfast and taking Jayce to school." I said. "No problem. I love you." She said putting her hand on my leg. I smiled "I love you too." We stared into each other's eyes for a moment. "I was going to ask you, do you have anything going on next Friday?" I asked. "No… Why?" she asked seductively as she smiled inching closer to my lips. "The girls from work are having a Halloween party, and they invited me. I was going to see if you would like to come with me." I said smirking as she was practically touching my lips with hers.

She put her soft hand on my cheek. "I think you should just stay with me Halloween night. I'll give you a private party." She said pushing me back down on the floor. She crawled on top of me whisking her long silky hair to one side like she always does. She sat on my mid-section as she gazed at me. I grabbed her thighs with a gentle grip. "That does sound quiet sexy, but I already told Donna I would be there. I don't like to ditch on people." I said. She laid down on me. "Not even for me?" she said in a serious tone. "Uhm…" I hesitated, something changed in her eyes when she said that. "It's not that I wouldn't for

72

you, I just haven't been out in a while so I figured..." as I was interrupted by Gracie. "What? You figured you could go and find a girl to bring home?" she said keeping the serious tone staying real close to my face.

I could feel her breathing on my lips from her nostrils. "That is not at all what I was going to say or do Gracie. Why are you acting like this?" I said getting defensive. It threw me off that she was getting emotional over something so stupid. I mean, I even invited her ass. She paused for a moment shutting her eyes turning her face away from me as she sighed deeply. "I'm sorry baby. I didn't mean to get like that." She said looking back at me. "It's just you are the best thing to have come into my life. I am really afraid of losing you." She said sincerely as her whole demeanor changed once again.

At that point I stopped holding my breath because honestly I was quite afraid. Especially her being on me. I was waiting to be choked or something. "Hey, I'm not going anywhere. Okay? I did invite you." I said. "I know, I know. I'm just being over protective." She said kissing me. "So are you going to come with me?" I asked. "I'm not much of a party goer babe. You go and have fun with your friends, then come back to me when you are done. I'll have something special for you." She said with a wink. "That sounds good." I smiled

Chapter 9

I arrive at the Halloween party. Donna runs right up to me giving me a big hug making my almost lose my balance. "I'm so glad you came! You look cute as a zombie." She said touching my stiff messy hair. "Thanks! You make a good looking Carrie." I said as I touched the fake blood on the white gown she was wearing. It was so real looking. "Would you like a drink?" she asked as she spoke loudly over the music. "Sure, a soda is good." I said. "Okay! I'll be right back." She said caressing my arm and running to the kitchen.

I take a walk around in the living room passing through the herd of people dancing having a good time. Her house was like a mansion, the living room is where she had the DJ set up with huge speakers that rattled the white marble floors. That room had to have at least sixty people in it. I didn't think that many people lived in this town. There were two cathedral staircases that let upstairs one on each side of the front room where you walk in through the door. She had a well-lit outside patio with a bunch of furniture. A hammock that was tied between two trees sat to the left of the porch. Donna comes back with quickness. "Here you go!" she says loudly. "Thank you!" I said taking a sip. "Your house is huge." I said loudly. "Yeah, it is pretty unnecessary. It's my parents' house." She said. "Do you live here with them?" I asked. "No, no, they are on vacation. They have no idea this is going on right now!" she said with a laugh. "Do you want to go out back so I can hear you better?" she asks. "Yeah." I said.

We walked out of the big glass sliding doors that had a frost outline of a huge rose on it. We sat on a white wooden swing that had a purple awning on it. "I am so glad you came." Donna says looking at me. She smelled like the fruity beer she was drinking mixed with some kind of perfume that had a cotton candy smell to it. It actually smelled good. "Yeah? I think you have already mentioned that." I said smiling looking at her. "Yeah! Well I meant it! I think you are really cool." She said. "Well thank you." I said smiling looking out at the big yard. There were a bunch of hedges that were carved into different shapes that lined a rectangular water fountain. "Did you carve those?" I asked being funny about the hedges. "Oh gosh no. My father does that shit. He is really into it for some reason. In the winter time he travels to New York to do ice sculpting competitions." She said like she was annoyed with him and his hobby.

"That sounds interesting. Does he ever win?" I said intrigued. "Yeah, he has won a few." She said. In the trees that line the side of the house, Gracie watches while listening. She clenches her fists drawing blood from the palms pf her hands. "You could come with us sometime." She added putting her hand on my knee. I pause as I look at her taking her hand off my knee kindly. "Sorry." I said politely. "What's wrong?" she asked innocently. "I am with someone. I thought you knew." I said in a serious tone. "With who? Gracie Lovely? Come on sweetie, you can do better than that." She said with a chuckle.

Gracie is getting more infuriated trying not to make a sound. As I sat in silence, it was starting to get awkward.

"Listen, I'm sorry, can we start over?" Donna asked. "Yeah, sure." I said feeling relieved. "Okay, good. I think you are too cool to lose." She said smiling. "Please make yourself at home." She said "I will be right back." She added as she walked inside to the bathroom.

I remain outside swinging by myself, until two co-workers of mine, Brandy and Crystal came over to me. "Hey! How is your lip?" Crystal asked. She was dressed as a playboy bunny with the white ears on a headband and a huge white cotton ball attached to her white booty shorts. She could definitely fit the part, she was so skinny like a twig and her hair was so blonde it almost looked white. She caked her make-up on as if she was hiding a bunch of acne scars on her face.

"It's better." I said chuckling. "That chick that came and took you, is that your girlfriend?" she asked. "Yeah she is." I responded. "Sorry, but she is kind of a bitch." She said laughing. I believe this was the chick that brought Gracie ice and a cloth when she asked for it. "She just cares a lot for me that's all." I said. "You know, I think Donna has a crush on you." She said. "Oh yeah?" I said already finding this out moments before they came outside.

I believe she was just trying to start shit so I tried not to pay into it. "Oh yeah! Like huge crush. You two should go out sometime." She replied. "But I am with someone." I said. Then the other chick, Brandy spoke up. If I had to guess she was dressed as a seductive cat. Her black shorts were so tight I could practically see the outline of her vagina. It looked as if her crotch was eating her shorts. Her hair was a dark caramel color just like her complexion.

"You're with Gracie Lovely? Well that bitch is a trip. She is a murderer." She said bluntly. "What are you talking about?" I said getting irritated with them both. "You haven't heard the stories?" she said sighing. "Um no. I don't buy into stories. I have to see it to believe it." I said sternly. "Well she is a psycho. You should give Donna a go." Brandy replied with sternness. "Thanks." I said as I got up to walk inside.

Meanwhile, Donna was in the bathroom fixing her make up on her face. A visitor walks into the bathroom with a black cloth mask on and a long black cloak that had a hood on it. They lock the door behind them. "Um Excuse me. I am almost done. Cute outfit by the way. Who are you supposed to be? The grim reaper or some shit? You know that is so out of date right?" She says laughing putting on her lip gloss as the masked visitor stands in silence. "Okay dude, you are starting to freak me out." As she looks at them in the mirror. She turns around to walk to the door. They stand in front of the door, pulling a knife out from their sleeve. "Oh, are we gonna play a Halloween game?" Donna asks sarcastically. The masked visitor shakes their head yes. "Okay but we gotta make it quick, I'm about to get my mac on downstairs with this fine honey." She says biting her lip.

The masked visitor pushes Donna into the tub with a very hard shove. Donna hits her head on the tub faucet. "What the fuck are you doing?!" she yells the music is so loud that you cannot hear her screaming for help. She touches her head where she hit, and feels the blood trickling down her scalp. "HELP!!" Donna yells. Donna

77

grabs the mask ripping it off the person. "Gracie!?" Donna says terrified. "Nicole is mine you nasty bitch." She says grabbing Donna's neck with one hand squeezing as hard as she could. Donna gasps for air and grabs Gracie's' wrist trying to get her to release. Then Gracie stabs Donna repeatedly in the stomach till she dies. Gracie gets up, leaving the knife stabbed in Donna's chest. She grabs the mask and puts it back on, unlocks the door walking out. I sit in the kitchen waiting for Donna to come back. It has been twenty minutes by now. I look around to see if I can see her. Then Crystal comes back up to me grabbing my arm.

Gracie keeps her distance in the crowd to where she can see me. She sees Crystal grab me as I yank away. Then a scream from upstairs overshadow the music. I run upstairs to see if it was Donna. Gracie slips out of the house as everyone is occupied with going upstairs. Everyone is crowded by the bathroom door. "What's going on?" I ask one of the guys standing by the doorway. He points into the bathroom as I can see Donna lying in the tub with blood splattered everywhere and a knife sticking out of her chest.

"That is some good special effect bro." this stoner kid Cam that was standing next to me says. I can hear murmuring from the crowd saying things like "Oh my god." and "Is she dead?" Brandy and Crystal look at me with tears in their eyes. "Someone should check her pulse." Brandy said in a shaken voice. "Why don't you?" Cam said with a laugh. "Are you too scared?" he added. "Fuck you Cam." She yelled. The cops are on their way." Crystal whispered in Brandy's ear as she put her arms around

Brandy from behind. I looked back at Donna's lifeless body in shock.

After a moment of no one taking the initiative, I took a deep breath walking over to Donna's body. I look behind me as everyone is watching me with suspense. I then look back at the body. I kneel down hesitantly inching my hand towards Donna's neck slowly to check the pulse. As I press on her cold neck, I felt nothing. I jerked my hand away quickly. I turn to everyone. "There is no pulse." I said. Brandy turns around to hug Crystal tight balling her eyes out. I turn my attention back to Donna, looking at the knife sticking out of her chest as I thought to myself how anyone could do this to someone else. I closed Donna's eyes with my index finger and thumb walking away.

I hear the sirens approaching the house as I open the front door; one of the officers draws his gun pointing it at me. "Don't move!" he orders me. I put my hands up scared shitless. "I didn't do anything." I said in a nervous voice. Some of the other guests come walking out as more officers draw their guns ordering us all to stay still with our hands up. Two officers run into the house and upstairs where Brandy and Crystal remained. "Alright everyone, I need you to line up single file." The officer said. There were about eighty people at this party so we formed a line across the front yard which was substantially huge anyways.

One officer inspected each and every one of us. He flashed the light in our eyes while we held our hands out. While another patted us down. "Has everyone been drinking?" the officer yelled to us. No one said a word. Then they passed a clipboard with a blank sheet of paper on it. "Write down your full name, address and phone number. You will each be called into the station for questioning and finger prints." He said loudly. That took three and a half hours.

While this was going on, Gracie sits in her bathroom naked on the edge of the tub with one leg crossed like a figure four. She has a razor blade in one hand as she is carving into the side of her ankle *GL + NS 4Ever* with a heart enclosing the initials. She doesn't even flinch once as she concentrates on making it neat as possible. You could hear the skin being carved off her smooth ankle. Her blood dripped on the white tile floor making a little puddle. She runs her foot under warm water then dries it. She walks to her office room and grabs a fresh ink cartridge from the printer. She cracks it open proceeding back to the bathroom. Taking the ink dabbing it on the fresh wound to make it permanent. She rubs the ink in and wipes off the excess. As she smiles to herself then kisses her ankle.

I arrive home later on that night. "You're home early." Kendyle says. "Are you okay? You look like you have seen a ghost." He said chuckling. I embrace him tightly. "Nick, what's going on?" he said sincerely. "There was..." I hesitated because I really didn't know how to explain it to him. I was shaken up by what I had experienced. "What's wrong sis?" he grabbed my hands softly. "Donna, that chick that invited me...well someone stabbed her to death." I said still in disbelief. "Oh my god!! No one saw??' he said concerned. "I guess not. I really don't know. Everyone was plastered anyways. She said she would be right back and twenty minutes later we find her in the tub…blood everywhere Dyle. Then I checked her pulse and nothing. Lifeless." I said starting to tear up. "Hey," Kendyle said softly as he pulled me into his arms to embrace me again "It's going to be okay." As he held me. "Did someone report it?" he asked. "Yeah that place was swarming with cops. They made us all write out names down before we left with our phone numbers. I will have to go in for questioning." I said listening to my brother's calm heartbeat. "If you want me to go with you I will." He said. "Then these two fucking girls were bothering me about Gracie, saying how she is a murderer. They don't even know her. They were trying to hook me up with Donna and I told them no man I'm with Gracie." I said getting angry lifting my head up to look at Kendyle. "We sis, sometimes people try to justify things they don't understand with rumors and lies." He said trying to calm me down. "I know it just makes me angry." I said putting my head back on his chest.

I have all these different emotions going through me right now. I was scared, angry, sad, and I just felt like I was spinning out of control inside. I've seen three dead bodies in the past two months. Kendyle held me tight as I tried to calm myself down. I closed my eyes trying to clear my head. "I don't want to sleep alone tonight. I'm going to go to Gracie's." I said looking at my brother. He softly said "Okay." His big brown eyes were glossy like he was holding back tears from me hurting. I know he hates to see me like this. He kissed my forehead and watched me walk to the bathroom.

I stood at the sink looking into the mirror. As I glanced down at my hands I suddenly had that feeling that I was dirty. Maybe it was because I touched a dead body or that for some reason I felt guilty. It hit me all at once so I took a long hot shower scrubbing my body till I was red like I had sunburn. I walk into my room to put on clothes. Gracie sits at her computer watching me with a vile smirk getting dressed. Since I leave my laptop open, she can see everything I do from my web cam.

I went to Gracie's letting myself in since the door was unlocked. "Gracie?" I said. The house was eerily quiet and dark. I walked around noticing a dim light from the computer room. "Gracie?" I said swinging into the doorway. No Gracie, then I proceeded down the hall. I came to the last room. I had my hand on the door knob when suddenly "Hey baby!" Gracie said from behind me startling me. "Geez girl, you scared the shit out of me." I said catching my breath with a smile. "I'm sorry." She said kissing my lips, putting her hand on mine that was on the door handle. "What are you doing?" she asks. "I was looking for you; I was going to see if you were in here." I said smiling. "I was doing laundry in the basement. I couldn't hear you calling me." she said innocently as she took my hand off the door knob to hold it walking me to the living room.

"How was the party?" she asked sweetly. "I don't really want to talk about it." I said following her to the couch. Gracie turned around quickly. "Were they mean to you?" she said angry. "No no, well I don't know just pushing I guess is the word to use." I said "Pushy?" she said still in a mean voice like she wanted to hurt them. "There was just a lot going on at the same time. It all happened very fast." I said. "What happened very fast?" she said lifting my chin up to look at her. "Uhm…Donna was stabbed to death." I said "That is horrible." She said petting the back of my head but there was such calmness in her voice. "It was crazy. No one saw anything. You would think in a house full of people someone would have saw something ya know?" I said still in disbelief. "It was a party baby, everyone was probably shit faced and not paying any mind." She said confidently smiling at me.

As I sat and thought for a moment. "I have to go in for questioning. They said they would call me in." I said looking at her. "I never had to do this sort of thing before." I said uncertain. "You have nothing to worry about. You are just an innocent bystander." She said still petting the back of my head. "How are you so sure? I could have done it." I said in a vile demeanor. "You are too collected for that." She said. "Plus most murders have fucked up minds. Maybe it was an angry customer or ex-employee." She said with confidence. "You are right; I couldn't do that to someone." I said smiling.

"What did you do this evening?" I asked trying to change the mood. "Just cleaned and did laundry." She said maintain a smile. "In the dark?" I said with a nervous chuckle. She laughed as she replied. "No silly. I was in the basement when you got here. No need to have the upstairs lights on." She said. "Want to watch a scary movie? They are on all weekend." She added trying to change the subject. "Yeah, that would be great." I said with a sigh of relief.

We walked over to the couch as I laid my head on her lap curling up in the fetal position. She played with my hair. "Is Jayce still having problems with that bully in school?" she asked innocently. "Actually he hasn't mentioned anything. Maybe you put fear into that boy." I chuckled. "Maybe." She smiled with content. She grabbed the blanket from the back of the couch and covered me up with it. She sat with a satisfying smile upon her face. She was practically putting me to sleep running her fingers through my hair.

What I did not know is while I was walking home from the party; Gracie went after Brandy and Crystal. They walked arm in arm giggling and staggering from the alcohol in the middle of a quiet road. Gracie followed far behind in the shadows. Brandy had eyeliner running down her face as they approached her house. "I'll see you tomorrow sweets." Crystal said as they kissed on the cheek. "Everything will be okay. And when they find that bastard who did this they will pay for their sins." She added as Brandy struggled trying to stand up hanging on Crystals arm. "I'm so fucked up right now." Brandy said giggling and crying at the same time. "I know, want me to come in." Crystal asked. "No honey, Brad will be home any minute, he's gonna be pissed at me." she said slurring. Brandy turned around shuffling her feet up the sidewalk leading to her porch. "Night sexy." Crystal said as she started her way farther down the road to her house in the village.

Crystal hears something behind her but as she turned around there was nothing. She mumbled to herself "Damn cats." As her breath dissipated into the late October crisp air. She crossed her arms as the temperature was getting colder outside. She then heard another noise but closer to her this time. "Hello?" she said hesitantly. "Brandy, if that's you this isn't funny." She said getting agitated. She turned back around and started to walk with more brisk pace. Then she heard running behind her. She didn't turn around she just began to run with her heels scraping the pavement. Then from behind her, Gracie still wearing the costume, grabbing Crystal covering her mouth stabbing her in the back then cutting upwards. "How dare you touch what's mine." Gracie whispered sadistically. As Crystal dropped to the pavement, Gracie dragged her into a bunch of bushes in the yard closest to them. Gracie turns Crystal around to look at her. Crystal chokes on her blood and spit while trying to speak. "This will be a lot quicker if you stop fidgeting." Gracie said stabbing Crystal in her right eye till the edge of the knife pokes through the back of her skull. Gracie then gets up leaving her there to bleed out.

Gracie walks to Brandy's house letting herself in through the back door quietly. Brandy is at the kitchen table passed out with her face lying in an empty plate full of bread crumbs. Gracie takes bleach from under the kitchen sink grabbing the back of Brandy's head leaning it back towards her. Gracie opens the bottle of bleach throwing the cap as it bounces off numerous objects in the room. Brandy tries desperately to open her blood shot eyes. Gracie has her mask off. "Well good morning sweetheart." Gracie says in an innocent tone.

Brandy becomes alert at that moment she sees Gracie's face. Gracie has a death grip on Brandy's neck as she pours the bottle of bleach down brandy's throat. Brandy struggles harshly to get away from Gracie's head lock grip. The way Gracie had Brandy's head tilted forced the poisoning liquid down her throat. "Bleach does a fantastic job of cleaning even the dirtiest fucking things. Especially things that like to talk shit about me to someone I love!" Gracie said gritting her teeth making sure to empty the bottle into Brandy.

Brandy starts choking up foam bubbling at the mouth. Gracie throws the empty bottle and pushes Brandy's body to the floor. Gracie takes a deep sigh. "That's better. The shit is all gone." As she exits the house whistling.

CHAPTER 10

I awake the next morning in Gracie's' bed. She lies next to me with her head on my chest and arm around my waist. Her room was always so bright in the morning. The one thing I love about living in Tenn. It seems the sun never misses a day to make an appearance. I look at the ceiling and listen to the birds outside singing away. It was a beautiful Saturday morning. I also had the day off it was glorious. The tight grip that Gracie embraced me in, so loved, like a barrier that kept me from harm. Then I got to thinking this is the second time she has carried me up the stairs to the bed. I did not realize I was such a heavy sleeper.

She inhales deeply and opens those beautiful brown eyes to look at me. "Good morning love." She says as she gently kisses my lips. "Good morning beautiful. Did you sleep well?" I asked "Of course. You're next to me." she said propping her head up on her hand to get a better look at me. "Do you feel better?" she asked softly referring to last night at the party. "Yeah, for now." I replied with uncertainty "You're off today right?" she says tracing her fingertips around my chest and in between my breasts. "Yes ma'am." I said with a smile. "Let's go somewhere." She said. "Okay. Where can we go?" I said since I was still uncertain of places around here.

"I can take you to Memphis. It's gorgeous there. They have a music festival this weekend. We should go and just take in the city." She said smiling. "Okay! That sounds great actually. I should go get some clean close first." I said. "You should bring your stuff here so you don't have to run home all the time." She said kissing my chest. I chuckled "Yeah..." I said unsure. "Okay well I'll be back in twenty." I said kissing her forehead getting up. "Hurry back." She said seductively as I stumbled out of the room.

Memphis was fantastic. I loved seeing the culture there. It just really made me love Tennessee even more. I could really get used to this place. We stayed at this cute little bed and breakfast right before you get into the heart of Memphis. As we pulled into the gravel driveway it looked like a house my grandmother used to live in back in the day. It was well kept with a white bench swing in the front yard. The house was light tan with a big bay window in the front. We walk in and the old man at the counter greeted us with a big southern hello. "How do you do folks?" he asked with a southern drawl. "We are fantastic!" Gracie replied with excitement. "I made a reservation this morning. Lovely is the last name." she said smiling touching my arm. I smiled back taking a look around. There was old style furniture that had that antique look to it. A floral day bed sat in the lobby with flyers neatly stacked on a white table next to it. It was so quiet there I could hear myself breathing. The smell of fresh paint was prominent. From the looks of the high vaulted bright white ceiling, I would say they painted it this morning.

"Ready sweetheart?" Gracie asked walking up behind me. "Yes." I said as I turned around to face her putting my arm around her waist. "So since you are still new to Tennessee, I am going to officiate you." She said with a giggle. "That sounds dirty." I said with a wink. "Only if you want it to be." She said moving close in front of me grabbing my shirt. "Mayybbee." I said with a grin. "I am gonna take you to have the best ribs you will ever eat in your life." She said smiling. "I am so down for some ribs." I said rubbing my stomach.

Thinking to myself as we were waiting on our ribs to be cooked at this southern restaurant. Ribs are messy; I may actually see this chick be not neat for once. I was excited to see how she was going to go about eating them.

As our waiter served us the platters they were huge. With a side of fries and coleslaw. Gracie looked at my plate. "Well, what do you think?" she asked. "I think that I am glad my brother is home and I get this whole thing to myself. He would definitely fight for these with me." I said with a chuckle. Gracie grabbed a rib and began to eat. I stared with a big grin. "What is so funny honey?" she asked with sauce on her lips. "Uhm..I never see you get messy." I said with a smile. "Oh, when I eat ribs, I eat them the right way." She said. "And what is the right way?" I asked being funny. "Like a boss!" She said with a giggle.

As we finished our meal, we took a walk downtown to enjoy the sights. I grabbed her hand to hold it as she clenched my hand to let me know she loved it. The festival started. There were so many people but it was a lot of fun. The band that was playing did a lot of blues and oldies. I love that stuff. I spun Gracie around in the crowd as we danced most of the night till our feet hurt. The way she laughed and danced with me had me feeling so happy. I didn't want this night to end.

On our drive home Sunday afternoon I thought it was a god idea to tell her about Sam. "My best friend Sam is coming up for the weekend." I said with a bit of hesitation. "Oh. Sam? Is that a guy?" she asked. I laughed "No. Sam is a chick." I said. Gracie's smile went to a straight face. "What?" I asked. "Is she your girlfriend?" she asked a little irritated. "What? No! We grew up together. Her oldest son is friends with Jayce too." I said. "Well why is she coming?" She asked a little more irritated. "Just to see the new place and to get away for the weekend?" I said "Are you upset?" I asked. She sat in silence for a minute before she answered me. She took a deep breath "No, of course not." She said forcing a smile.

"You really do have a little bit of a jealousy issue huh?" I said getting a bit irritated with her. "No." she short answered me. "Yeah. That's why you are giving me the short answer treatment now. Listen Sam and I have been best friends for over twenty years. I never once thought about Sam in a sexual way. Just my friend that is all." I said sternly. "Baby." She said pulling over the car. She took my hand in hers. "I know. I am sorry. Let's just not ruin this perfect weekend okay?" she said so innocently. I took a deep breath to let out the frustration. "Yeah." I said as we continued home I stared at the road for the rest of the way.

Chapter 11

Kendyle sits in his office with one hand resting on his head as he tries to make sense of a case he has coming up. Calvin walks in. "He bud, me and a couple others are going to lunch, you want to joins us?" he asks. "Ummmm... Yeah sure I'll tag along." Kendyle says relieved. They go to a little diner in the city, carrying on about everyday things escaping their stressful work day. "So Kendyle, how do you like it here?" Mary asks. Mary is a tall skinny blonde that always looks her best even on her worst days.

She speaks intelligently but still manages to pull off the dorky girl. "I like it here. It's beautiful and the street we live on is quiet which is a big plus." Kendyle replied. "So where did you buy a house at?" Mary asks. "Sunset Valley Road." He said. Mary, Calvin, and another fellow co-worker Liam look at Kendyle as if he said the scariest place on earth. "What?" Did I say something wrong?" Kendyle asks with a nervous smile hoping they were just messing with him. "Miss Lovely lives on that road if I'm not mistaken." Calvin said. "Yeah, yeah she does. Right across the street actually." Kendyle said taking a sip of his tea.

The table remained quiet for a few moments as Kendyle began to wonder why they seemed like they knew something he should know. "You guys want to share something with me? Or are you just going to look at me like I'm a ghost?" Kendyle asked in a serious tone. "Have you met Miss Lovely?" Mary asked. "I have. She seems very nice and cool. My sister hangs around with her." Kendyle says. "Do you know anything about her?" Mary asks. "Not much other than she is really neat and clean.

And a little odd at times, but we all have our days I guess." Kendyle added. "My sister tells me when she goes over there it always smells like Lysol or some kind of clean smell which is a very good thing." Kendyle said. "Probably to mask the smell of the dead bodies in the basement." Liam said under his breath. "What?" Kendyle looked at Liam. "Nothing, it's just I've heard stories that's all." Liam added and went back to eating. "What kind of stories?" Kendyle asked looking at the three of them. "You guys are freaking me out. If there is something I should know, I want to know. I mean my sister is around her constantly. If I should be concerned please enlighten me." Kendyle says.

"Well, there is this one I don't know what you would call it. Story I guess..." Calvin says leaning in towards Kendyle to keep the conversation quiet. "They say when she was a little girl she would do unusual things when she was upset. For example when she didn't get her way, she would set fire to her dolls in the kitchen. Then one night she tried to suffocate her mother with a pillow while she was sleeping but the father caught her in time. So her parents thought she needed help. They were going to send her to the Western Mental Health Institute but the next morning after the decision was made, her parents found that little Gracie was nowhere to be found. It was like she knew what they wanted to do with her. So she ran away from home at age nine. Her parents didn't even make an effort to search for her. And it wasn't until a couple of years ago she showed back up. Mainly to claim her parents' house or she would have lost all the inheritance. But while she was missing that's when odd things started happening." Calvin explained. "What kind of weird things?" Kendyle asked being very engrossed in all of this.

"Well, like the death of her parents and a few others. Her father was a very wealthy man. He was a well-known mortician around here and also owned his own flower business along with some of the other businesses around this town. Some say he was murdered by an angry customer but I fondly believe it was Gracie. They never found his body. But they did find fingerprints of a man whose wife had passed away a week before. They said the man was angry with the way Mr. Lovely made his late wife look and went off on a rage killing Mr. Lovely. Then her mother committed suicide a year later hanging herself from an upstairs bedroom window. Or so they think she did." Calvin added. "Do you think the mother killed herself?" Kendyle asked. "No way! That lady was the sweetest woman I have ever met. She would have never harmed an ant little lone herself. I'm sure Gracie did it to gain all the family assets such as that nice house and money. Gracie is the only known family member still alive. Did she tell you what she does for a living?" Calvin asks. "She says she works from home… selling flowers." Kendyle replied thinking to himself now.

Calvin smiles and leans back in the chair. "There you have it." Calvin said. "Just because she works from home doesn't mean she is a killer." Kendyle says trying to ease himself more so. "Okay, then explain this one. That house that is for sale next to your house. An old couple used to live there years ago when this all started. They were really good friends with The Lovely's… The Wilsons.

They became too suspicious for their own good. One day Mr. Wilson went over to the house just to "check" on things. So he found his way into the house and noticed a lock on the basement door. Why would anyone keep a lock on a basement door?" Calvin said. "Scared of the basement." Kendyle said justifying the reasons. "Good guess but no. Mr. Wilson found two decomposed bodies in the basement behind this wooden door down there that at one point was chained locked. He said it smelled like rotting roadkill the closer he got to it. That, my friend, is why her house always smells so clean. One of the bodies he claims was the "angry customer" that supposedly killed Mr. Lovely." Calvin said. "How do you know all of this?" Kendyle asked. "Because the Wilsons...were my grandparents." Calvin said. "I'm sorry. I had no idea." Kendyle said. "No it's okay; just I think Gracie got them too." Calvin said looking at Kendyle. "But why?" Kendyle asked. "Because my grandfather was nosey and my grandmother was just aware of what was going on. " Calvin said.

"Gracie does not like to leave any loose ends. She is smarter than she puts on. Do not let that pretty face fool you my friend. Calvin added. "May I ask how they passed?" Kendyle asked hesitantly. "My grandmother was already sick. She was on a breathing machine. The doctor said she suffocated from lack of oxygen like it was cut off at some point the day she passed and my grandfather; well he fell down the stairs breaking his back. A splinter from his spine punctured his heart. But I firmly believe he was pushed by the psycho bitch. "Calvin said getting angry. "I don't know what your realtor told you, but there have been

94

quite a few families in and out of the house you are in. I just think it makes sense. Gracie gets too attached to someone, and then... well I think you know." Calvin added. "Just be careful, and your sister. Gracie likes nothing in her way. So my advice, either move, don't be nosey or kill the bitch." Calvin said.

As the table got quiet and awkward, Kendyle began to think of the story on the news about Kristen, how she drove off a bridge. Did she really? Or was this a devilish act of Gracie trying to rid anyone in the path of her getting close to Nicole.

Meanwhile back at the Shaw's' house, I begins to unpack a few more boxes. As I am going through the box with my picture frames in it. I pick up the one that Sam and I are supposed to be in and noticed it missing. I mutter to myself. "Where did it go?" I'm searching feeling confused as to what may have happened to it.

I call Kendyle to ask him if maybe he saw it in the trailer or just around somewhere. "Hey!" I said "Oh hey sis? Is everything okay!?" Kendyle asks worried as he is still shook up buy the stories he heard a bit ago. "Yeah everything is fine. I was just unpacking some before Sam gets here and noticed some of my pictures are missing. Have you seen them?" I asked. "Hmm I don't remember seeing any. Did you put them in a different box?" he asked. "No I don't think I did. Or maybe I did and just do not remember doing it." I said second thinking it. "Well I'm sure we will find them. I'll help you look when I get home." Kendyle replied. "Okay bro... and this may seem like a weird question but do you know what Haloperidol

95

is?" I ask. It was bothering me ever since I found it in Gracie's' drawer. I just wanted to know what I was dealing with. "Yeah, that's a psych drug used for mental patients." He says as Calvin looks at him with concern. Kendyle looks at Calvin. "Why do you ask?" Kendyle asks hesitantly.

"I found some in Gracie's dresser drawer, I was just wondering what it did." I said sorting through the box not surprised by his answer. Kendyle stays silent as he thinks of everything he just heard from Calvin and now this. "Are you alone right now?" he asks. "Yes. Why?" I chuckled. "Just wondering. I'll be home early again today." He said with more concern in his voice. "Are you okay Brother?" I asked as I could sense something was off with him in the tone of his voice. "Yeah everything is fine." He said assuring me. "Okay, I'll see you soon." I said getting off the phone. Calvin stared at Kendyle waiting for him to say something. "Everything kosher?" Calvin asked. Even though he already knew things would fall into place for Kendyle now. "Yeah everything is good." Kendyle said holding his fist to his mouth in deep thought.

Soon after, I hear a car pull into the driveway. It's my good friend Sam. I run outside happy to see her, giving her a big hug. "Oh my god! I missed you" Sam said squeezing me. "I know me too! Are we sad or what?" I said laughing.

Gracie watched from her living room window behind the white laced curtains. She dug her fingernails into the window pane clawing the hard wood leaving deep scratch marks until her fingers bled. Gracie walks to her bathroom. She looks in the mirror gripping the sides of her white porcelain sink. Her blood dripped off her fingertips running down the sides to the floor. She starts breathing heavy. Her eyes well up so she looks down closing her eyes trying to calm herself. "FUCK!" she yells as she pulls the sink away from the wall. She stands still looking at the plaster torn off the wall. "Shit." She says under her breath. She calms down pushing the sink back on the wall to make it look like no harm done. She wipes her frustrated tears off her cheek smearing a little trapes of blood below her eye. A knock at her door snaps her out of it. She runs to the kitchen trying to wash the blood from her hands. "Just a minute." She says loudly. As she scrubs vigorously.

A knock again at the door hurries Gracie. She grabs a towel wiping her hands walking to the door. Gracie keeps her hands covered with the dark green dish towel. She swings the front door open a little irritated. "Hey." I said. Gracie's aggravated face turns quickly to a happy expression. "Hey honey." She says kissing me on the cheek. "You must be Sam." Gracie says cupping her hands together with the towel still covering them. "Yes I am." Sam said holding out her hand to greet Gracie. Gracie looks down at the towel and back up at Sam and I. "I...My hands are a bit greasy at the moment sorry." Gracie said with a vile smile. Sam puts her arm down "Oh no worries." Sam said delightfully. "Is everything okay? You seem tense." I said to Gracie concerned. I see a red line under her eye. I go to wipe it off. "What's this?" I said as she beat me to it wiping it off with towel in her hand. "Oh, that's nothing. She said looking frantically at us. "So what brings you over?" Gracie said with a deep breath. I stood confused for a moment. Something felt off, like there was tension in the air. "I just wanted to introduce you to my bff. We all are going out to dinner later. Would you like to join us?" I asked. "I'd love to." Gracie said forcing a happy smile.

Later on that evening, after Kendyle arrived home. "Is everyone ready to go?" he asked as he walked into the living room. Gracie turns around to look at Kendyle. "We are." She says with a grin. Kendyle stops dead in his steps. "Are you tagging along?" Kendyle says surprised. "If it's not a problem." She replied. Kendyle looked at me then back at Gracie. "Not at all." He says faking a smile. "Good." She says holding Jayce's hand walking him to the car.

On the ride there, Kendyle keeps his eyes on Gracie in his rearview. "Are you sure you don't want me to drive?" I whisper to Kendyle. "I'm okay. Why?" he snaps out of it looking at me. "You seem distracted." I say concerned. He smiles at me not saying a word.

We all enjoyed a dinner in the city. Gracie sat quietly listening to the story Sam was telling but not really taking it in. Kendyle watched Gracie from the corner of his eye nervously. "Dyle, you okay?" I asked again. "Huh. Umm yeah just a long day." He replied "Do you want to talk about it?" Sam asked. "Not really." He said and sipped his beer. "So Gracie, what do you do for a living?" Sam asked being intrigued by how pretty and proper Gracie seemed. Plus Sam sometimes talks about herself a little too much. I think she was getting the hint. "I work from home selling flowers." She answered. "That sounds cool. Do you do all the arrangements and everything?" Sam asked even more intrigued "Yes. All of it. I have a greenhouse in my backyard for them." Gracie answered quickly as if she didn't want to talk. "I would love to do something simple like that while Don and the kids aren't home." Sam said talking to all of us. "It's not that simple." Gracie said offended. "I didn't mean it like simple as in easy I just meant..." As Gracie interrupted "You have to be really good at making things pretty, paying attention to detail. From the looks of your wardrobe and hair you're not good at either." Gracie said rudely. "Whoa! Where did that come from?" I said a bit embarrassed.

Kendyle stared at Gracie as she caught him. That's when she knew he had an idea of who she was. "Thank you for inviting me, but I must be going." She said sifting through her black suede purse for her money. "Here is for my portion and yours. Enjoy your night." Gracie said as she kissed me inappropriately jamming her tongue down my throat at the table as she shot Sam a vile look then walked out. "That was very odd. I'm so sorry Sam" I said. "It's okay." Sam replied as she seemed very confused. "Should I go after her?" I asked Kendyle. He shook his head no. As I could see he was fuming. "But we drove her here." I said. "She can catch a taxi." Kendyle said firmly.

Later on we arrived home. "Aunt Sammy" Jayce said "Yes Sweetie" she replied want to play a game with me. "He asked. "Sure!" she said as Jayce grabbed her hand while running to his room with her. "Guess I'll be back later "She said with a chuckle. "Nick!" Kendyle said "Yeah." I replied walking into the kitchen. "What's up?" I asked crossing my arms. "I think you should stay away

99

from Gracie for a while." He said hesitantly I giggled and responded. "Why? Are you jealous?" Jokingly. "No it's not that. I just have been hearing some things." He said looking down the hall to make sure Jayce and Sam were occupied. "Things?" I said confused. "What kind of things?" I asked. "Just..." he moved closer "That she is not the person we think she is." He said sincerely as to not piss me off. "Brother, I love you and I know we don't get to spend much time but I promise I'm not going anywhere. Okay?" I said thinking it was a separation anxiety thing for him. "No I know you're not I just ...don't want to see you get hurt." He said grabbing my arm gently. "Hurt? As in falling for another dumb girl?" I said with a chuckle. "Something like that." Kendyle said.

My brother has always been very logical and never jumped to conclusions unless he knew the facts of something. That's why he makes such a great lawyer. "Listen, I'm going to be careful this time. I promise." I said kissing him on the cheek walking to Jayce's room. Kendyle glanced across the street from the kitchen thinking to himself. As we all got ready to turn in for the night, I gave Sam my room and I slept on the floor in Jayce's room.

Sam gets up in the middle of the night to use the bathroom. She is half asleep but notices the shower curtain moving slightly as if there was a draft or a light wind coming from the window. She thinks nothing of it. She walks over to the sink to wash her hands. From behind her Gracie grabs Sam's' mouth and injects a siring into her neck. "Now that's simple bitch." Gracie whispers in her ear as Sam can only struggle for a few seconds till she is out

100

cold. Gracie pushes Sam's lifeless body through the bathroom window letting her fall to the ground breaking her neck. "Ooops." Gracie said with a smile dragging her to her house by the hair. Gracie then proceeds to drag her to the basement and hoists her into a large freezer under the stairs locking it.

Gracie proceeds back over to our house to get Sam's car. She puts it in neutral rolling in over to her house placing it in her garage along with her belongings. The next morning, Kendyle wakes me and Jayce. "Are you two going to sleep all day or what?" He said as he walked down the hall. "Okay buddy you ready?" I said stretching. "Yeah." Jayce said rubbing his eyes in a sleepy manner getting out of bed. I knocked on my door as to not wake Sam abruptly. She didn't answer me so I open the door to see all her stuff gone and my mattress made neatly. "Sam?" I said. Kendyle comes back in. "Have you seen Sam?" I said "No. But her car is gone. Why?" Kendyle replied. "All her stuff is gone like she up and left. She wouldn't do that without a goodbye." I said confused. "Well maybe there was an emergency back home. I'm sure she will text you soon." Kendyle said walking back outside. I approached the door to see Gracie making her way over with a tray of cookies.

She walks up the porch stairs handing me the tray. "I feel so bad for my behavior last night. I made these as a peace offering for you and your friend." She said with that innocent tone along with a smile that would make you forgive her in a heartbeat. "Well thank you but Sam left I guess." I said a little disappointed. "Awe. Why? I hope not because of me." Gracie said "I'm not sure. I woke up and she was gone." I said putting my head down. "I'm sure there is a perfect explanation for it." Gracie said shoving the cookie tray towards me to take it. "Peanut butter?" I said with a smirk. "Yes." Gracie said with a smile. "My favorite." I replied and took the tray to set it in the kitchen. Gracie followed me inside the house. Kendyle walks in "Gracie." Kendyle said startled. "I'm really sorry for my behavior last night. I made cookies for you all. I just have been having a rough week." She said placing her hands behind her back. "Haven't we all." Kendyle said. As he walked back outside. "Is he okay?" Gracie asked turning to face me. "Yeah. He's been acting a little strange since yesterday. I think he misses Ashley though." I said. "Can we go somewhere to talk?" Gracie asked. "I'd like that. Is it okay if I bring Jayce? Kendyle is occupied. I don't want to stress my bro out more than he already is." I said. "Of course." She said with a smile, as we walked down the road.

Kendyle watched as we turned the corner way down at the end. He ran to the backyard of Gracie's' house in a paranoid manner. Searching frantically for a way in. He glances at the greenhouse that looks like it hasn't been used in years. The outside is not kept up at all. Nature looks like she is reclaiming it as her own. He runs over to the greenhouse quickly. The door is pad locked shut. He runs to the side to see if he can see through the scratched up plastic windows. Upon looking inside, he is taken back by the desolate look of the inside of the greenhouse. There was very tall grass growing inside along with grape vines and weeds growing all up the sides of the walls. Moss filled each corner. To himself he whispers "No fucking way." He takes a picture with his phone, then runs back to the back porch.

He approached the sliding glass doors pulling his license out from his wallet. He slides it between the door and the latch unlocking the door. He helped himself in as he stood at the door looking around. He noticed how clean and immaculate the house was. He glanced down at his shoes taking them off as he walked briskly through the house looking for the basement door. He turned the corner to go into the kitchen. He noticed a bottle of sleeping pills on the counter next to a jar of peanut butter.

Meanwhile Jayce, Gracie and I walked enjoying the weather. "So what did you want to talk to me about?" I asked putting my arm around Gracie. "Well I just wanted to tell you that I love you so much. I hate when I wake up and you are not next to me." Gracie said gazing into my eyes. "Well duh. I knew that." I said laughing. "When your sister in law comes home, you are more than welcome to stay with me." She said as I stopped and faced her. "Do you think that's moving a little fast?" I asked a little concerned. "Not at all. You love me and I love you, I just thought we could get closer." She said keeping a smile. "Listen, I know you are close with your brother and Jayce, but it's just across the street. You can visit them anytime. "She said grabbing my hands. Jayce is busy picking daisies in the yard next to us while we have this conversation.

Kendyle still frantically searches for the basement door. He sees an out of place door under the stairs as he approaches it. He notices it is locked. "Bingo." He says under his breath. He walks to the kitchen to find something to pick the lock with. Sifting through the drawers under and beside the kitchen sink. He runs to the front of the house to look out of the big bay window to see if we are on our way back yet. Upon seeing nothing he runs back to the kitchen searching more. He is sweating so much that the collar of his shirt is soaked.

Jayce goes up to Gracie. "I picked these for you." He said handing her the hand full of daisies. "Thank you Jayce, they are beautiful." She said kneeling down to him. "You are the only girlfriend of mine he has ever liked it's weird." I said Gracie looked up at me standing back up. "Girlfriend huh?" she said moving closer and kissing me.

Back at the house, Kendyle notices a door ajar in the hallway. He walks over to it to see what's in there. As he opens it he is instantly taken back by all the pictures taped to the walls of his sister. "What the hell?" Kendyle says under his breath as he walks in farther in the room. He sees pictures from when they were outside playing football a few days ago. Some of her sleeping and some when she was getting dressed. He walks over to a table that has a shirt that looks very familiar as he picks it up he notices it's one of mine. Then under that is a pair of panties that have been worn and a picture that was photo shopped that he knew he took a few years ago of Sam and I. In the place of Sam's face was covered by a picture of Gracie. "Holy shit." He then sees a toy heart that looked very familiar. He picked it up and knew it was what Jayce had given me years ago. There was a bloody washcloth folded neatly next to all of that from my busted lip. "This is really happening." He says to himself. He backs out of the room walking out quickly.

"Aunt Nicki? I have to go to the bathroom." Jayce said dancing around. "Okay buddy lets go." I said grabbing Gracie's hand heading back to the house. Kendyle found a small screw driver that fit perfectly in the lock. He popped it open and opens the door. "Ughh! God!" he said as a rotted stench bombarded his nostrils. He put his nose in the crease of his arm turning the flashlight app on his phone. Seeing the light switch did not work, he walked down slowly. The cat bolted downstairs "Fuck!!" Kendyle yelled. "Jesus, damn cat." he said catching his breath laughing. Gracie, Jayce and I turn the corner walking back down to the house.

Kendyle looks around following the rotting smell. He sees the door that Calvin was talking about yesterday at lunch. Then he shines his light over to the right and sees the big freezer with blood drops on the top. "Damn, this bitch locks everything." He said picking up the lock on the freezer. He sticks the screw driver in the lock and pops it open. He hesitantly opens it slowly. As the steam cleared he saw Sam's body. "Shit. Shit!" he slammed the door down. Frozen from shock he stood looking at the freezer in disbelief out of breath. Gracie, Jayce and I walked into our house. Jayce runs to the bathroom. "Where is your brother?" Gracie asked calmly as she knew something was off. "He should be outside." I said looking out in the back yard. "Shit." Gracie said "What's wrong. "I forgot to feed Cloud this morning. I'll be right back." She said walking briskly out the door. "Okay." I said.

105

Kendyle made his way back upstairs locking the lock back on the basement door. He hears the door knob being unlocked. "Fuck." he said under his breath as he scurried to the glass sliding doors grabbing his shoes. Sliding the door shut quietly just as the front door opens. He jumps of the side of the deck putting his shoes on running back to his yard. Gracie walks briskly through her house. She walks down the hall to her shrine of Nicole and notices the shirt was moved. "Damn it." She says slamming the door. She walks back out to the front of her porch and sees Kendyle moving boxes in his garage. He turns around to see Gracie staring at him. He smiles and waves. "You coming over to help?" He says like nothing happened. She walks back into her house slamming the door. Kendyle smiles and walks into the house.

CHAPTER 12

"I have to talk to you like now." Kendyle says grabbing my arm leading me to his room. "Kendyle! What's going on with you? You have been acting really strange the last two days." I said yanking my arm from him. "You have to listen to me, and I know how farfetched this will sound." He said looking me in the eyes. "Okay, what is it?" I said "These people I work with told me things about Gracie that I didn't want to believe. So when you guys went for a walk I went into her house..." I interrupted him "You broke in??" I said angry punching his arm. "I had to see if they were messing with me or not. "He said "Well what stories were they telling you??" I said getting irritated. "That she killed people." He said "Now you sound like them bitches at the party. Gracie is way too nice to be a killer." I said in disbelieve. "I know! That's why I thought they were messing with me till I found things…" he stopped as to he didn't know how to tell me that my best friend was one of the things he had found. "What things? Like dead bodies?" I asked "Yes." He said sincerely.

He had this look in his eyes that I knew he had something he had to tell me but didn't know how. "If this is your attempt to keep me from getting hurt again this is a really sick way of doing it Kendyle." I said getting angry again. "I'm not making this shit up." He said grabbing my arms to keep me still. I was moving away from him because I wanted to punch him for saying these things. Gracie was so sweet I just could not believe any of this.

Meanwhile Gracie hears the cat meowing as she tries to call him to her. "Cloud, where are you?" she says as she walks the house looking for him. She turns the corner getting closer to the basement door as the meowing gets louder. Cloud is clawing at the basement door as Gracie looks at the lock. She walks sternly to her bedroom getting the key. She slams her dresser drawer closed, walking angrily back to the door. She opens the basement door, picking Cloud up and kisses his head. "Awe buddy, why were you down there." She says evil eyeing the house across the street.

Back at the Shaw's house, Kendyle tries to desperately convince me of Gracie's' vile ways. We stood there silent for a moment. "Nick, I wouldn't make something like this up. Listen I know you really like her and I do too, but I think there may be something not right with her head." Kendyle said. "I understand you are doing the big brother thing, and I love you for it. I just think before you go jumping to conclusions..." Kendyle interrupted me and blurted "She killed Sam." He said fast. I paused. "What?" I said in disbelief. "I found her body in the freezer in the basement." He said softly. My eyes welled up. I knew he was telling the truth because of how he said it. I always could tell when he was lying to me. He would always have a weird little smirk he could never prank me. "Oh my god..." I said gasping, putting my head in my hands as I started to weep.

Gracie made her way back to our house as she knocked on the door frame. "Nicki?" Gracie said innocently. I turned around abruptly wiping my tears. "Hey." I said like nothing was wrong. Kendyle stared at Gracie as she walked over to us. "Is everything okay?" She asked putting one hand on my lower back. "Umm yeah everything is fine." I said sniffing the snot back into my sinuses. "It doesn't look like everything is fine." She said as she glared at Kendyle from behind my back. "We are fine here." Kendyle spoke sternly. "You should come over. I will ease your sorrows." Gracie said petting the back of my head. "I think I just need to be alone for a while. I'll come over later." I said holding back the tears looking at Gracie. "Okay, well you know cookies make will make you smile." She said as she kissed my lips with her eyes open looking at Kendyle.

She approached the door while looking over her shoulder. She gave Kendyle a deranged grin. Then proceed to fade into the sunlight. "You can't go over there. She knows!" Kendyle said nervously. "I have to or she will think something is up." I said wiping my cheek of a lingering tear. "Just tell her you fell asleep or have the shits for Christ sake! She knows that I know. If you go over there she will not let you come back..." He said looking me in the eyes intently. "I mean it Nick, until I can figure out what to do about this to keep us safe." He said kissing my forehead and walking outside.

I took a deep sigh looking at the tray of cookies. I walked over to it, picking three up walking to my room as I indulged. Kendyle stared at Gracie's' house. Then he ran inside. "Nick, I think I have an idea…Nick?" he walked to my room as I was passed out in a deep sleep on the mattress. "Nick?" he said shaking me. "Wake up." he said softly. "Shit." He said running into the kitchen seeing a few cookies were gone. "Damn it!" He said to himself. He ran back into my room. "Nick you have to get up! Nick!" he said shaking me franticly but no avail. He made sure I was breathing properly and covered me up.

The sun was sinking slowly in the days end. Kendyle planned on going over there early in the morning to get evidence to have Gracie put away. He hoped she would be asleep by this time. He put Jayce to bed later that night. "Okay buddy, I have to go somewhere in a little bit and I want you to stay in bed okay. Auntie Nicki doesn't feel well but she is in her room. Okay?" he said innocently to Jayce. "Okay daddy. Where are you going?" he asked "I have to go help Gracie with something." Kendyle said tucking Jayce in. "Can you tell her that she should come over tomorrow and play in the pool with us. " Jayce said. Kendyle paused and smiled at Jayce. "I'll mention it buddy. I love you." Kendyle said kissing Jayce and closing the door.

Kendyle lied in bed wide awake till 3:30 watching the clock. His nerves were shaky with knots in his stomach. He got up walking to my room in hopes that the sleeping pills wore off. "Nick." He said quietly as to not wake Jayce. I didn't move a muscle. He walked briskly to Gracie's back yard as he looked up at the windows making sure all lights were off and there was no movement. He walked slowly up the porch, once again pulled his license out to unhinge the door. He was shaking with nervousness and his hands were so clammy he could hardly keep grip of the license. The first swipe he did to unhinge the door from the latch was unsuccessful. "Damn." He said quietly.

110

He took a deep breath and did it again. This time his license slipped out of his hand and down through the gap in the deck where the wood lied next to the next piece of wood. "Fuck!" he whispered. He took his wallet out of his back pocket thinking do I dare try a credit card. But he needed the proof that Gracie was a murderer to have her put away so he and his family could live safely once again. So he pulled a credit card out of one of the slots in his wallet, wiped his hand on his shorts and tried once more. This time he succeeded. He waited a moment to see if he had made too much noise, he was in the clear. He opened the door as slow as he possibly could, taking his shoes off at the door as to eliminate some noise walking through the house. He shut the door behind him quietly.

He walked to the kitchen to find something else to get the lock open with since he dropped the screw driver in the basement after his discovery of bodies. He saw the bottle of sleeping pills still on the counter by the peanut butter. He was curious as to how many she possible crushed up into the batter of cookies. He picked it up and it was empty. He looked in the trash to see a brand new box torn open. "She used the whole damn bottle." He said to himself. "Crazy bitch." As he set the bottle back down. Kendyle couldn't find anything else in the kitchen to get the lock open with so he moved on to the living room searching for the door leading to the garage.

He found it upon walking through the living room into a mud room. He slowly opened the garage door. It squeaked slightly as his heart was pounding out of his chest he stopped and listened for footsteps. Nothing was heard so he squeezed his skinny self through the ajar opening that was made. He turned the flashlight on his phone to look around. Besides Gracie's car was Sam's vehicle as well. Kendyle looked at it for a moment, sighed and shook his head in disgust. He took a picture of both cars next to each other. Then proceeded to look for something for the lock. He saw a pair of small bolt cutters lying on the ground under a work bench off to the side that was very dilapidated like it hasn't been used in years. He crouches down and picked them up. "Nice." He said walking back into the house leaving the door the way it was as not to let it squeak again. He walks over to the basement door keeping an eye out just in case. He puts the cutters around the U of the lock and takes a deep breath. As the chain rattles slightly he cuts the lock as it falls to the floor. "Fuck." he mutters to himself as he hides in the living room as to be certain she heard that.

He hides behind the couch listening for footsteps once again. He's soaking his shirt in sweat and swears his heart is about to explode in his chest. His ears are ringing and he cannot control the shake his body is producing. He stays in this position for over fifteen minutes. He hears nothing. He is confused, and thinks maybe she used the sleeping pills for herself. Maybe it was a coincidence that Nick was in a deep sleep. He gets up peering over the back of the couch looking around in the shadows of the full moon shining in from the big bay windows in the room. He sets the cutters down and walks over to the basement door again.

He opens it putting the collar of his shirt on his nose as he walks down the stairs quickly but quietly. He shines the light on his phone to see the freezer. He opens it trying to ignore what's inside. But upon opening it, Sam's body is gone. "What the fuck did she do with it?" he mutters to himself. He looks at the wooden door he remembers Calvin telling him about. He walks over to it and notices the lock is unlocked. He takes his shirt off his nose seeming perplexed. When he goes in for the handle he hears footsteps on Gracie's front porch. He runs up to the top of the basement stairs, grabs the lock and chain shutting the door. He hears footsteps walking on the wooden floors in the house going upstairs as they stop midway. A thud, then footsteps comes back down slowly.

Kendyle walks down the stairs quietly holding the chain and lock as still as possible as he searches for somewhere to hide. The basement door opens; he hears footsteps coming down the stairs. Kendyle hides in the corner on the other side of the freezer crouching down in hopes that he will not be seen. He closes his eyes and grips the chain as the footsteps get closer to the freezer. He mouths the words "Please god." As he looks up at rafters that have insulation hanging which also are covered in cobwebs and black mold. The footsteps stop at two steps away from the side of the freezer he is hiding at. A big black spider crawls briskly across Kendyle' arm as he desperately tries to keep it together. He bites his lip and clenches the chain tighter. The sweat from his hands and body start to trickle to the cement floor. Then the footsteps scuffle back up the stairs then the door slams.

Kendyle gasps for air after holding his breath the whole time. He drops the chain down and wipes the spider off of him smashing it with his foot. "UGHH!" he lets out a big sigh. He sits quietly till he hears no more movement. He sees a small window at the one end of the basement that he could fit through. He walks over to it, trying to push it open. It's like it has been sealed shut. It's one of those windows that you can't see in or out of it looks like ice. He tries tapping it with the lock he had cut to crack the glass. "This is going to take forever." he says to himself. He makes his way back up the basement stairs. He opens the door very slowly and peaks around to see if he can make a run for the back door. He steps out closing the door behind him tip toeing to the back door where he came in at. He grabs his shoes, sliding out. Running home, he leans up against his front door in the house catching his breath.

CHAPTER 13

Kendyle walks to my room opening the door slowly. "Nick." He says walking over to the mattress. "Nick." As he pulls the covers back it's just a pillow there. "No!" he says getting up abruptly. He runs to Jayce's room and sees he is fast asleep. He gets ready to run out the door then decides to get a weapon of a sort. He runs outside to his car, popping the trunk. He lifts the fabric up to the spare tire area and grabs the tire iron. He then runs over to Gracie's opening the front door which is unlocked. He holds the tire iron up getting ready to swing, he creeps in. "Nick." He whispers. "Nick are you in here?" He whispers again. Looking around franticly. The moonlight makes a path through the hallway leading to the back door. "Nick?" Kendyle whispers again.

Meanwhile I wake abruptly like I had a bad dream. My head was pounding so I massaged my temples. "Ughh man." I mutter to myself. I hear Kendyle's voice in the distance. "Kendyle?" I say in a normal but confused voice. I sit up. "Nick, where are you?" Kendyle says a little louder this time. "I'm up here." I said in a normal tone. Kendyle runs upstairs. He finds me in Gracie's' bedroom with my ankle chained to the metal bed frame. "Thank god." he says running over to me hugging me tightly. "We have to go." He said. "My ankle hurts." I said looking to see a thick shackle around it. "What the hell?" I said scared. "She must have carried you over here while I was in the basement." He said looking at me with the only light from the moon shining on my face. "What happened?" I asked. "She crushed up sleeping pills and put it in the damn

115

cookies." Kendyle said. "That is some psycho shit! How am I supposed to get this damn thing off of me?" I asked nervously grabbing my ankle. Kendyle stands up and hits the frame of the bed with the tire iron at least a dozen times.

"Wait wait!" I said grabbing Kendyles' wrist. "What?" Kendyle says. "She's up here." I whispered and grabbed Kendyles' arm. I could feel her eyes on me, but the house had so many dark corners it was hard to pin point which one she was in. "I'm not going to let her hurt you." Kendyle said "There are bolt cutters downstairs. I will be right back I promise." He said handing me the tire iron, running downstairs. "I will wait here." I said humorously. I stood by the window scared for my life. In fact, I think this is the most scared I have ever been. I was shaking so bad that my teeth were chattering. I gripped the tire iron as tight as I could, getting ready to swing if I had to.

Kendyle runs to the couch but the cutters are no longer there. "Looking for these?" Gracie said behind him in a sadistic voice. He turned around as she swung hitting Kendyle in the head with them knocking him to the ground. "Kendyle!!" I yelled from the room as I could hear the loud thud. Kendyle tried getting up to go to the kitchen as he staggered Gracie followed close behind. "You crazy bitch." Kendyle said holding his head. "You know, I tried to be a friendly caring neighbor and you just wanted to be a nosey one. I do not like that. You should have just minded your own fucking business. I thought your little work friends gave you a heads up." Gracie said. Walking around the island in the middle of the kitchen. "You're a sick woman." Kendyle said breathing hard as he leaned himself against the kitchen counter trying to stand.

She cracked her neck and glared at him. "My mother used to call me sick, look where that got her." She said continuing to walking around the island in the middle of the kitchen. She was trying to get to Kendyle as he moved the other way. "I love your sister but you just cannot let us be. That's another thing I do not like. She is mine Kendyle. Mine." Gracie said getting very defensive. "She doesn't like psyhco bitches." He said as Gracie jumped across the Island at him. She grabbed his shirt practically ripping it off. He grabbed a knife that was on the island in a chef block. He sliced Gracie's' arm as she let out a yell. "Mother fucker!" she said. He took off to get to the upstairs but Gracie grabbed the back of his head yanking him to the ground. "I don't think so bitch." She said as Kendyle lied on the floor holding his head in pain. It was pounding from the hit he took to the head a second time that his vision was a little blurry.

She walked around Kendyle body, grabbing his jaw turning his head to face her. "If you would have let things take their path, none of this would be happening right now." She said calmly with a smile as she pushed his head the other way standing up.

While this is happening, I try taking the shackle off my ankle by slipping it over my foot. "Fuck!" I yell as it's too tight to fit over the bones in my foot. "Baby, I'll be there in a minute. Don't be doing anything you are going to regret later." Gracie yells up to me. "Nick!!" Kendyle yells in agony. Gracie covers Kendyle's mouth with her hand.

"If you value your tongue, I wouldn't speak if I were you."
She said smiling. "Dyle!?" I yell to my brother. I could tell
he was in tremendous pain.

I use the tire iron to beat the frame of the bed but it
would not budge. With tears in my eyes, I'm getting more
frustrated. "Shit!' I say to myself. Then I try using my heal
stomping on the frame but I just end up bruising myself. I
grab the frame of the bed pushing it to the door frame. It is
too wide to fit through the door.

Gracie picks Kendyle up from under his arms
dragging him to the basement door. The whole right side of
his face is covered in blood from the bolt cutters hitting his
temple. She drops him to the ground yet again causing him
to hit his head. She reaches in her pocket for the key. "You
know, you own me a new chain and lock by the way. These
things are not cheap. I had to run to the store today to buy
one, and do you know how much this fucking thing cost
me?" she said looking down at Kendyle as he rocked back
and forth holding his head on the floor. "Twenty five
fucking dollars." She said swinging opening the door to the
basement. "Fuck...you..." Kendyle muttered with anger.

Gracie laughed kneeling down to Kendyle "That is
probably not the best thing to say to someone who basically
is about to take your life." She said as she grabbed him
from under the arms again getting ready to thrown him
down the stairs. He tried to grip her wrist as he bit her as
hard as he could. "Ahhhh!!" she yelled and grabbed his
neck. "Fucker!" she yelled as she threw him down the
stairs. She looked at her wrist and back at Kendyle lying on
the cold concrete floor. "Now that will leave an evil taste in

your mouth as you fucking die!" She screamed slamming the door shut putting the new chain and lock on it.

She walked to the kitchen as she could hear me beating on the frame upstairs. "Baby, what did I tell you?" she said loudly so I could hear her. I stopped and fell to the floor as it was exhausting me to the point where I was running out of energy. Gracie ran her bloody wrist under water for a few moments and wrapped it up with a cloth bandage from the bathroom. She took the key out of her pocket and placed it in the junk drawer in the kitchen.

She reached for an eighty percent alcohol bottle of tequila that sat in her cupboard. She walks over to the laundry chute as she says to Kendyle. "We could have made this work. You are a good guy Kendyle. But, you like to keep Nick all to yourself. I cannot have that. She is a grown woman." She says dousing a wash rag with the tequila. Kendyle lies painfully at the bottom of the stairs listening to Gracie rambling on. "Oh, and just so you know I will take care of Nicki and Jayce since we have to get rid of you now. In fact I think it's time for me to get rid of all the memories in this house." She says pouring some tequila down the chute as it hits the floor and some clothing that was hanging to dry on a string down in the basement.

She stuffs the rag that she doused in alcohol then lit it on fire throwing it down the chute. The flames catch on some of the clothing on the way to the cement shattering on the ground. "Nick!!" Kendyle yells not being able to move much from all the pain he has just endured. Holding his ribs with one arm and reaching for the stair banister to hoist himself to stand. "Nick!!" he yells again in pain.

Gracie walks slowly up the stairs. I could tell just by the way she was walking up the stairs that there was something evil with her. The footsteps of a cold blooded killer was about to be standing in front of me. I hid under the bed. Not like I thought she wouldn't see me, I just didn't know what to do. I couldn't get loose and I didn't know where the key was. I needed a moment to think. "Baby." She said softly. "I think it's best if we go now okay?" she says as she kneels to the floor to see me under the bed. "What are you doing silly." she said grabbing the tire iron from my grips. I held it as tight as I could but she grabbed my wrist and pried my fingers off. They were so sweaty I couldn't keep a firm grasp on it. Those beautiful eyes that I thought were filled with love and warmth were now filled with darkness like I have never experienced.

She then threw my weapon down the hall then crawled on the bed to get to the shackle since I pushed the bed blocking the door frame. She pulls me gently towards her by my feet. I roll over on my back. I sit up to look her in the eyes. She unlocks the shackle then holds my hands. "Come on, don't be scared." She said forcing an intimate kiss on me. She held the back of my head still with firmness. She helped me up. My heal hurt really bad from all the stomping I did trying to get loose. She put her arm around me as we walked slowly down the stairs.

I was trying to think of a way to knock her out or something so I could get my brother. My mind was going a million thoughts a minute. It was really hard to focus on one thing. "Nick!!" Kendyle yells again as we are making our way down the stairs. I look at Gracie as we stop midway. His voice triggered something inside of me. "Just ignore him baby. He doesn't want you to be happy. That's not fair." She said as we started to near the end of the stairs I give her one good push with all my energy I had as she falls six stairs down knocking her head on the wooden floor. I run to the basement door. "Kendyle! Where is the key?" I said frantically. "Uhm...she has it on her....just get a screw driver or something…" Kendyle tried to remember as everything is still fuzzy. "You have to hurry bro!" I said looking back at Gracie as her foot twitched. "It's the drawer in the kitchen." He said. "Yeah! Which one!? There is like twenty!" I said "The one closest to the sliding doors." He yelled as he started to choke from the smoke that was over taking the basement. He pulled his way to the top of the stairs with the help of the banister. The fire was crawling up the walls to the insulation on the basement ceiling. "Hurry Nick!" Kendyle yelled as he watched the flames grow.

As I sifted through this junk draw I look behind me to see if she was still on the floor but she was gone. "Shit." I said under my breath as I turned my focus back to the drawer. I found a key that had a B on it with permanent marker. It looked as if it was freshly put on there so I'm guessing it was the right one. I hear a creek close behind me. I take a deep breath and close my eyes.

Gracie came up behind me slowly putting both her hands under my arms running them up my chest to my breast. One single tear fell silently from my left eye. She kissed my neck giving it a gentle playful bite. She whispered in my ear "We are meant to be together forever.

You are mine. Do not make this difficult. I love you more than anyone will ever love you." My heart was beating so fast I thought I was going to go into cardiac arrest. I opened my eyes and glanced down. I see scissors that were in the junk drawer. I grabbed them, turning around abruptly stabbing her in the stomach. Stunned we both stand there in shock. I could not believe I just did that and she probably thought the same. She held her stomach where I stabbed her. She took her hand off the wound looking at the blood covering her hand. She then fell to the ground.

I run to the basement door as I am shaking trying to get it open. I get it unlocked and Kendyle practically falls into my arms. Black smoke rushes out of the basement. Kendyle gasps for air, I put his arm around my neck and we make an attempt to get out of the house. Gracie steps in front of me. "I forgive you for stabbing me baby. I know love can be a scary thing, but I will never hurt you." She says walking towards me with one closed fist like she was hiding something in it. "Please don't do this." I said trying my hardest to hold Kendyle up. He was all dead weight at this point. "I know this is hard for you honey, but I will make life so beautiful." She said still walking towards us slowly forcing me to walk back to the staircase leading upstairs.

We stand at a stalemate for a few moments as the fire started to take over downstairs. I could hear the floor boards starting to creek and pop. "This place is going to collapse. You have to let us go." I said in tears. "We can go baby, just you and I." she said "No, he is coming with me." I said sternly holding Kendyle closer to me. "Fine." She said as she lunged at me forcing me to drop Kendyle to the ground as she knocks me to the floor as well.

Gracie lays on me on the ground forcing herself upon me putting her hand around my neck. "We are perfect together! Why do you not see it as I see?! I don't like it when you misbehave. I want you all to myself. We belong together!" Gracie says forcing two pills in my mouth holding my tongue as they slide down my throat forcing me to swallow them. I was trying desperately to push them out. But the more I struggled the more I felt them slipping in the back of my throat down my esophagus. She lets go, getting off of me running off into the darkness.

I turn over on my side. I stick my finger in my mouth trying desperately to puke up the pills. I cough and dry heave trying to get them to come up. I even punch my stomach a few times to help the reflex. I finally managed to upchuck to shrunken pills knowing that some of it has dissolved in my system. I try to regain my strength. I feel slightly groggy, and my muscles feel really at ease. I crawl over to my brother.

The blood drips from the right side of his head. "Kendyle, wake up. Kendyle!!" I said with tears in my eyes. I put my head on his chest then hear a scream from across the street. It's Jayce yelling for me. I gather up all I had left in me. Picking up Kendyle, I hop over to the house. I lay Kendyle in the hedges to keep him hidden. "I'll be right back brother I promise." I said kissing his head laying him on his side.

I carefully watch my back as I go into our house. I grab the bridge of my nose for a moment and stand still. I started to feel dizzy and my stomach was rumbling. I proceed into the hallway. "Jayce buddy, where are you?" I said as I look out our back door I see him standing by the edge of the pool as a get closer Gracie is right next to him. She looks very upset with tears in her eyes. She had a red face with eyes like she had been crying. She was overly frustrated. I open the door. "Please don't hurt him. " I said reaching for him. "Want to know how I learned how to swim?" Gracie said biting her teeth together as she said it very angrily. "No!" I said as she pushed Jayce into the deep end of the pool. I quickly dove in after him.

Kendyle woke up trying to sit up. He could see the black smoke barreling out of Gracie's house. He sees Gracie running back to her house to the backyard. He stayed low as to not be seen. I get Jayce out of the water as he gasps for air. "Buddy breathe!" I said to him petting his head holding him close to me. "It's okay. I got you." I said rocking him back and forth till he was able to catch his breath. I looked around in alert watching for Gracie to pop out at any minute. "Be very quiet." I said to Jayce as we made our way back into our house to get my phone. Jayce and I stayed in the dark as I called the cops. I could see a shadow outside next to where I left Kendyle in the hedges.

Kendyle stays on a lookout but still no sign of Gracie. He hears a crunch of grass behind him as Gracie chokes him with a piece of garden twine. When I'm on the phone, I hear Kendyle trying to yell. I hand the phone to Jayce. "Tell them everything. Stay here!" I said running

124

outside. Gracie is dragging Kendyle by the twine around his neck back to her house. Kendyle tried to get his fingers between the twine and his neck gasping for air. She manages to drag him all the way into her house again. "Just die you bastard!" she yells in his face with frustration. The floor of the house is becoming more dilapidated by the minute. The paint on the walls is starting to drip and the wooded floors are charred and weak.

I run over to Gracie standing in the doorway. The floor beneath Kendyle and Gracie is starting to break and cave. "No Nick, stay there!" Kendyle mutters still trying to catch a breath. He holds his hand out like he wants me to stay where I am. "Yes baby stay there this will only take a second." Gracie says dragging Kendyle by the twine still trying to get him to the basement again.

The basement now looks like the pits of hell. Any thought I ever had of what hell looked like, that's what it would be. The smell of the rotting reminisces filled the air. The basement is engulfed in flames, and the house is filled with smoke I can barely see a thing. I step lightly with care through the house to get to them. Kendyle holds the basement door frame as tight as he could. "Stop you asshole!" Gracie yells in Kendyles' face again. He spits in her eyes. She tightens up on the twine. "That wasn't very nice." She says calmly but gritting her teeth.

I finally make my way to where they were. "Gracie." I said calmly with tears in my eyes. "Yes dear." She looks at me and smiles. The burnt orange color from the flames jumping out of the basement door illuminated her face. I glance at Kendyle struggling to keep his grip on the frame as Gracie is still trying to get him to let go by pulling on the twine, pressing his hand down with her foot. I hold my hand out to her. She gave me that big white smile, and in that moment, it was the way I wanted to remember her. "Time to go home." I said smiling with tears in my eyes. She instantly let go of the twine and reached for my hand. Before she could grab onto me Kendyle popped up pushing himself off the floor grabbing Gracie from her waist throwing her into the basement of flames. We closed and locked the door with the chain. "Come on!" Kendyle said putting his hands over my ears to muffle the sound of Gracie screaming for me. I stop in the road collapsing to the ground.

I lay my sweaty body on the cold pavement. I close my eyes and just breathe. Kendyle laid beside me holding me close as I cried in silence. We lay in the road, watching the house crumble from the inside out. We were both covered in dirt, soot, and sweat. Kendyle kisses my head as his embrace got tighter. I squeezed his arm trying to ease my heart rate.

We hear sirens in the distance as Kendyle pressed his lips on my forehead. I still cry in silence as we watch the house diminish. Jayce comes running out of the house. "Aunt Nicki!" he says as he falls into my lap with happiness while I sit up. Kendyle embraces us both as two ambulances and three firetrucks approach us.

They put Kendyle on a stretcher and nursed his wound on his head. Jayce and I hop into the back with him as they drive us away. I stare out the window of the ambulance as we leave our street. I felt so drained and

numb. Kendyle takes my hand. "Hey?" he says softly as I
turn to face him. "You are the best." He added with his big
white smile. I grin with watery eyes and nod my head yes.
"So are you." I said letting out a sigh of relief. I kiss his
hand and put my arm around Jayce as he lays his head on
my side. "Why do you always go for the psycho bitches?"
he asks laughing but holding his ribs in pain. "I think I have
it all out of my system now." I smiled. "Let's hope so. I'm
pretty sure I cannot handle another one after all of this." He
says humorously. "Yeah…me neither." I said with a grin.

Thank You

I would like to thank all of you who took the time to read this novel. It means a lot to me. Most of all thank you to all that support my writing and Team Ayce. You guys rock.

Ayce

www.ingramcontent.com/pod-product-compliance
Lightning Source LLC
Chambersburg PA
CBHW060633130626
46555CB00002B/785